Borderline

Jenny Morris

LEAF BY LEAF

Published by Leaf by Leaf
an imprint of Cinnamon Press,

Office 49019, PO Box 92, Cardiff, CF11 1NB
www.cinnamonpress.com

The right of Jenny Morris to be identified as author of this work has been
asserted by her in accordance with the Copyright, Designs and Patent Act,
1988. © 2021..

Print Edition ISBN 978-1-78864-931-5

British Library Cataloguing in Publication Data. A CIP record for this book
can be obtained from the British Library.

Designed and typeset in Adobe Jenson by Cinnamon Press.
Cover design by Adam Craig © Adam Craig.
Cinnamon Press is represented by Inpress.

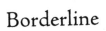

Borderline

For Josephine and Jeremy, with thanks

March

Eve had been given away as a child.

She thought about that every time she saw or heard a baby. And that day in March a child was crying nearby. A long drawn out, hopeless wail that caused her to stand still, listening.

In the large Victorian house, the main entrance door slammed. Curious, being new, she went to her window. A hugely fat man came out and shuffled across the parking area towards the street. He was bald and wore tight beige jogging trousers and a sweat top. From her turret she saw him as a series of slowly progressing, bulging circles. When he turned to pause at the wall, she could see just how short he was. He coughed. Now she knew he must be the one who lived on the floor under hers, the one who climbed the shabby stairs so laboriously and wheezed so much.

Somewhere in the house the child stopped crying.

In the silence someone rang the bell on her internal front door.

She glanced at the mirror. Her light hair hung in tangles round her shoulders, her jeans covered in paint stains and her feet bare. She pulled a demented face, not wanting to see anyone, wondering if she could pretend not to be in.

Her bell chimed again.

She'd learned in a few days that in this converted old house the walls of the flats were thin. Neighbours could tell who was at home. She didn't want to offend anyone yet.

She opened the door.

The tall figure on the landing blocked out the light. 'How do you do? I'm Hester Monkman. Welcome to Strand House.' She wore a black, wide brimmed hat over her black dyed, cobweb profusion of hair. A dark coat dropped from shoulders to doormat. Hooded, sharp eyes and a narrow, high-bridged nose gave her the look of an eagle. A thrust-out hand gripped Eve's fiercely.

She winced and stepped back. 'Hello, I'm Eve Key. Do come in. I'm afraid it's a bit of a mess.' She caught an odour of whisky and nicotine. 'Coffee? I've just made some.'

'Ah,' with a glance round, 'you don't know what serious mess is.' Hester's face, a slightly crumpled parchment, trembled. 'Black for me.'

While Eve fiddled with the brewed coffee she tried not to stare at her guest. Hester stepped round the small apartment with the air of a sergeant-major on inspection. The outcome was favourable. 'You've done wonders. The couple who lived here before were anoraks into twitching, spent their time lying in mud on the marshes. They liked the colour of sludge.'

'Yes, some walls took four coats of white paint to cover it.'

Hester picked her way round a pile of boxes. She took a cigarette packet from her pocket, looked at it, sighed, then put it away again.

Eve didn't say anything. She poured coffee into a mug. 'Which part of the house do you live in?'

'Ground floor. Number one. By the front door. It's useful for the dogs.'

Eve hadn't heard any dogs, but there were a couple of cats in the house. They lurked on the stairs and were easy to fall over in the gloom. 'I thought the lease said no pets.'

'Ah, that.' Hester breathed in heavily. 'As long as everyone is agreeable, animals are fine. I couldn't live without my labradors. They love the beach.'

Eve thought of small children playing in the sand among dog mess.

Hester stuck out her bottom lip and shot imaginary smoke towards the ceiling. 'Sadly, from the beginning of May until September they're banned on the nearest beaches, poor darlings. So then we have to go further afield. But they've just

8

had a marvellous fortnight on the moors, running around all day. I'm only just back from visiting my son. Otherwise, I'd have called on you earlier. I spend most of my time out with the dogs. Or writing. I've been a widow for years.' She grinned, exposing crooked yellow teeth. 'You may have heard of my late husband, the writer, journalist and soak. He was big in Soho. The drink got him. Liver shot to pieces. I'm writing about him. *My Life With Hugo*. It's been on the go for ages. I can't decide what to put in and leave out. If I don't finish soon everyone will have forgotten about him. He covered wars, famines, met celebrities. We had many bizarre nights.'

She looked at Eve.

The young woman had the feeling that she was about to be quizzed on her own life and wanted to forestall that. 'Who lives directly below me?'

'Number four? That's Amos Postle, short and fat. Born in this town, works in the little ironmonger on the High Street. Shy. A bit deaf. Sensitive about his size. He's been looking for a wife for as long as I've known him. Does internet dating, goes off on mysterious assignations.'

'I've met the man adjacent to me on this landing. Number six. The one with the bleached busby hairdo, Darren.' He was tall and emaciated and ran lightly up all the flights of stairs making scarcely a sound. 'What does he do?'

'Not much. Drugs, sometimes, I fancy. He does work at the crab factory on and off.'

'He seems to be out at night a good bit.'

'Goes to the club by the bus station like all the youngsters round here I expect. There's not much else.' Hester reached out to the windowsill and picked up the framed photograph of a young girl in school uniform. 'Nice eyes, very white shirt. Who's this?'

'My daughter, Jez.'

'Is she going to school here?'

'No. That was taken a while ago. She's not with me.' Eve put her hand out for the photo and carefully replaced it.

'Where is she then?'

'Round the world trip. Backpacking.'

'With a friend?'

There was a silence.

'No.' Do shut up, woman, thought Eve.

'That's brave. But I did something similar myself in my teens.' Hester rubbed her grubby fingers. 'Dancing with danger... But I must go and unpack the old Morris Traveller. It's a treasure, an antique. I'm absolutely petrified it will give up the ghost soon. I pray for it, nightly.' She drank down the remains of her hot coffee and pushed her shoulders back. 'Splendid to meet you, Eve. Vast improvement on the boring bird lovers. And thank you for the coffee. Can't stand the instant muck. You must come to my little get together tomorrow night. Drinks at eight?' She smiled and left in a hurry.

As Eve watched the top of the black fedora lurch downstairs, Darren came running up, his silver earrings glinting.

'Awright, mate?' His smile was lopsided and genuine.

'Fine. You?'

'Great.' He dashed into his flat leaving the door ajar.

All the time Eve had been in Strand House, Darren's front door had been left open displaying a pile of magazines and dirty washing.

As she pulled her own door to and the Yale lock clicked, she heard the rhythmic, relentless boom of heavy metal on the other side of the wall.

Would Jez like that music now?

Since Eve's move from London, she'd so much to do. Her new part-time job due to start after Easter needed organisation. But she missed her daughter.

Picking up the photo taken nine years earlier, she sighed

at the familiar depiction of that clear, ingenuous gaze. Now Jez was lost to her mother.

A mother can't be with her children forever, Eve thought, can't always be there urging them to eat properly and not go too near the edge with drugs or alcohol or chancy partners. You just let them go and hope. At a young age Eve herself had wandered near the edge often. She shuddered. That was the trouble, the unstoppable risk-taking and craziness of youth.

Jez was short for Jezebel, a name chosen by the pagan, teenage Eve for her daughter as soon as she'd set eyes on her, dark haired and red faced, waving her fists in a London labour room. A female of spirit, decided Eve. She had always secretly admired that scheming, shameless Jezebel since first reading about her in school. And anyway, there was no one to deny her that choice.

But the little girl turned out to be a most gentle child, kind and obedient, a fish-eating vegetarian at eight and one who certainly didn't care for her name.

'I'm Jez. That's short for Jessica,' she explained firmly on the first day at her secondary school, and told her mother later. There she conformed to the rules and, at weekends, joined the local church choir and organised Harvest Festival hampers for the old people of the parish. She was never timid, but always curious about other people and different ways of life.

Eve felt guilty at the choice of name for her only child and every time she recalled the black ink inscribed on the birth certificate, twisted her mouth and groaned. Poor Jez. Somehow her name must protect her from all dangers.

And now she was so far, so lost to her. Eve stared at a single, fat, red tulip in a glass vase on the mantelpiece. She'd found it in the park, snapped off in the wind. It's closed up like a heart, she thought, like mine, cool and still. It's just a lost thing, something that exists and then dies and decays.

And who's to know or care?

She stood at the dormer window and looked out at the sea. Beyond the rooftops it stretched in shadowed bars, glistening in places where the sunlight filtered through clouds. The white flecks on the waves were reflected in a hail of blossom, torn early from the trees, which flurried up against the glass to be swept away.

A scent of salt was suspended inside the attic room. It was cold.

Her decision had been swift. She chose to move to a small town on the North Norfolk coast because she had never been there and accommodation was cheap. Her escape. After selling her London studio flat there was enough money to buy something similar in Shipden, enough for a year's travelling with some left over to allow Eve to live without full-time teaching. A great bonus, allowing her to paint.

The north light in the living room was ideal. The newly painted white walls shone with reflected radiance from sea and sky. At the top of the old house, the past servants' quarters, her windows faced in three directions. The views had persuaded her to buy the flat: to the east, the avenue and other divided mansions set in tended gardens, and at night, the rhythmical beam of the lighthouse, to the north the sea beyond the park and boating pond, and to the west the first shops and restaurants and the massive church tower rising above rooftops and chimneys.

She thought the town quaint with its elegant Georgian and Victorian terraces, its terracotta facades and odd domes, its flint stone fishermen's cottages, and its old-fashioned little butchers and sweet shops where everyone spoke politely and parcelled up purchases neatly. The pace was reassuringly slow. This must be a good, safe place in which to live.

Touching the cold red tulip in passing, she went to her computer. There was an e-mail from Jez. As the words appeared on the screen she smiled.

Mum. Are you settled? I logged on this morning for the first time in seven days and have heaps of messages, which is good as I have spent the last night in the most squalid, vile place you have ever seen in your life. It was the cheapest of course. The complete and absolute pits and as it was my first night in Singapore, I am trying hard not to let it put me off the city. The room was filthy and the ceiling falling in. The water from the basin ran straight out into a bucket underneath. The cockroaches were gigantic. I left at 5am past the snoring Chinese man at the bar. Otherwise, the city is great. It's really clean and you can't chew gum or eat in the streets. I'm enjoying ambling around and eating strange food in the hawkers' stalls. I like the Indian doughy bread and some big spiky fruit I don't know the name of. There are all sorts of exciting dishes such as Pigs' Organ Soup and Chicken Feet With Noodle, which I am avoiding, but I accidentally ate some sort of animal thing last week in Bali which sorted out my constipation problem. You will be pleased to know that I am cleaning and flossing my teeth regularly as I can't bear the thought of being in the middle of nowhere with toothache. Lots of love Sweaty Jez with mozzie bites xxx

Eve tapped out a response:

Jez. This place is great. The sea air makes everything look clean and sparkling. It's amazing after dirty old London. I haven't had a chance to start my own artworks yet, I'm still sorting out painting walls and enjoying myself arranging stuff. Am sleeping better here than I've done for years. My neighbours are odd. There's Amos, a strange little fat man living below who's like a troll in a fairy tale, and below him an oldish woman called Hester who's a kind witch. I'm growing my hair really long to hang out of my turret window for the handsome prince to climb up, eventually. I've had fish and chips every night since I moved here. Can't get enough. Mm. Glad to know that you're taking care of yourself. Lots of love, M.

She needed to buy food, and so went out to explore further.

The breeze rushed from the North Sea. She recalled a London friend telling her how the weather tended to be 'bracing' in Norfolk. I need to be braced, she thought, wishing she'd put a jacket on, and walking faster.

Newly painted shop windows were full of Easter eggs and paper flowers.

People smiled at her in passing. Some strangers even greeted her. One can't be inconspicuous and anonymous in a small town, she mused, I'm too used to city living.

In a newsagent's, she read the headlines about a girl who'd disappeared on her way home from school in a city suburb. There were pictures, the girl smiling, in her uniform. Innocent eyes, short hair, a rumpled white collar. There was something about that dishevelled choirboy collar that made Eve sick.

Eve imagined the worst of what might have happened and what her family was going through. In her head she saw an area cordoned by police tape. She stumbled as she meandered along narrow pavements, passing strangers, stepping off into the street, nearly getting knocked over by a van. She headed for the sea, shivering.

Under a washed-out sky, electricians hung coloured lights along the front as rusty tractors dragged two-man crab boats on hawsers over the sand and shingle.

She stopped to watch the boxes of shellfish being unloaded, then went along the pier where a man with a thermos guarded fishing lines. The café-bar and little theatre at the end were being renovated for holidaymakers. Everything was waiting for the action.

The next evening at half past eight Eve, wearing a red dress and carrying daffodils, walked down the wide flights of stairs in Strand House. Going by various doors, one marked 'A. Postle' in faint pencil letters, she knocked on the white entrance of number one.

As the door opened a noise of conversation and a smell of smoke and dogs hit her. She held the flowers to her nose before offering them to Hester, who, encased in black, ushered her into the living room.

'Everyone, this is the new occupant of number seven. Do welcome Eve!' Hester turned to a table of bottles and an old lady leaning on a stick. 'Bloody Mary.'

Eve wasn't sure whether this was an introduction or a drink suggestion. 'Mm.'

She accepted a huge glass of what turned out to be mostly vodka.

'Baskets, boys!' Hester pointed. Two dark and shiny dogs were sniffing about, waving their tails and knocking over small china objects. They padded with reluctance into the kitchen.

The sparse-haired lady with bright, knowing eyes peered over her spectacles. 'Pleased to meet you, Eve. I'm Grace Tombling and that's my husband, Vernon, in the corner. We're at number two across the hall.' She fumbled with her stick, a glass of sherry—rivulets sliding down the outside— and an outsize handbag. 'So difficult to manage.'

Eve helped her into a chair next to a windowsill adorned with pots of primulas. 'The garden is lovely here.'

Grace beamed. 'I'm so glad you like it. Vernon and I do all the gardening at Strand House. We're very particular. Some plants don't do well by the sea, but the earth is rich. The roses are beautiful in summer and the hollyhocks. He cuts the little bit of grass and the hedges, but he doesn't have as much spare time as me. I only help in the charity shop by the church, but he works for people with learning difficulties. He just can't retire.'

Eve stared at the sprightly figure of Vernon, amiable and bloodhound-jowled, who vigorously handed round crisps.

'Aha. This must be the new resident.' A faint foreign

accent. Authoritative voice.

She turned as a tall, bone-thin man put his arm round her shoulder.

In a leather jacket and jeans, with long, black, untidy hair and dark stubble, he appeared self-assured, with deep-set eyes scrutinising her from head to toe, well-defined Pharaoh lips in a sensual curve. 'I'm Choker.' He extended his hand.

'Something Choker? Or Choker something?'

'Neither. It stands alone.'

'Do you live in this house, too?'

'No. My place is the other side of town. But I'm often here, visiting Hester. Mine's the motorbike round the side.' He looked down her front. 'I like your frock. Very pleasant.'

She pulled up the low-cut bodice slightly and gulped her drink.

'What do you do, Eve, tempt?'

'Not at all,' coldly. 'I teach art history.' She told him about the part-time job she'd been offered at the city college.

'How will you get there?'

'By train. They seem to run frequently.'

'Not often enough, you'll find.' He refilled his whisky glass. 'I used to teach. Given it up now, thank God.'

'Choker's a poet,' said Hester, in passing. 'He has several slim volumes.' She paused. 'And you know what poets are like. They have triple compulsions—getting published, getting drunk, and having sex.' She patted his cheek.

In the silence that followed Eve stared at the floor. 'What things, er, what do you write about?' she asked.

'Someone once said that there are only three subjects for poems: love, death and time. I prefer death.'

At that word she thought again of the missing girl whose parents she'd seen on television appealing for information. Why hadn't the girl come home? Eve thought about Jez. Her eyes blurred. 'Excuse me.' She walked across the room.

The walls had built-in bookcases from floor to ceiling.

They contained mostly old books, gilded and soft coloured. Eve pretended to study one and blew her nose. She looked around. The ceiling was stained with nicotine and the long curtains were a faded crimson brocade. Intricately patterned cotton nets had turned bone coloured in years of sunlight. A large, worn, Persian rug covered the floorboards and little mahogany tables were littered with porcelain animals and pot-pourri dishes.

Amos had squashed himself on a sofa next to a girl with an infant. He quivered, red and perspiring, ill at ease. 'What?' he kept shouting to the girl. His voice, high-pitched, belonged to a different person.

Eve introduced herself.

He didn't look her in the eye. 'I saw you move in. Lots of pictures.' He struggled to rise. 'I'm just now going,' he said. 'Got to go.'

He stood less than five feet tall, but bulky. As he tipped his head back in his effort to get away, the hugeness of his nostrils showed. She noted the plump apples of his cheeks, the sparseness of eyebrows and lashes, the almost lipless mouth, the comparative smallness of his hands and feet, and a scent of mildew clinging to his clothes. He was, she felt, afraid of her.

As he bulldozed to the door, she sat in the unpleasantly warm seat he'd vacated.

'Cheers,' said the girl with waist length copper hair in braids. She crossed her long, bare legs, one with a tattoo of a butterfly on the ankle. 'I'm Cheryl and this is my Troy. He's eighteen months. Don't talk yet but he been running around since he was ten months.'

This must be the child I heard, thought Eve.

Troy lay propped against a cushion, almost asleep, a dummy plugging his mouth. He looked a sturdy boy, his dark hair shaven to the top of his ears. His eyelids flickered and closed.

Cheryl pricked his cheek with a purple talon. 'At least you int going to be a nuisance.' She turned to Eve. 'He don't sleep a lot, usually.' She seemed annoyed he'd chosen that time for a nap.

Eve had noticed his buggy in the hall earlier. 'Which flat do you live in?'

'Five.'

'That's the first floor, isn't it?'

'Yes. Above them moaning old Tomblings. They're always complaining about Troy. He have a little car he sit in and they say it make noise on the floorboards. Poor kid's got to play somewhere. They don't like my music either.' She gave a hoarse bark of laughter. 'I don't give a stuff.'

'My daughter would probably like your music. She's about your age.'

'She got any kids?'

'No. She's travelling at the moment.'

'Will she come here after? To Shipden?'

'I'm not sure. For a while perhaps.'

'She'll bloody hate it. It's dead boring here. Nothing to do. I bin here all my life. Three pubs worth going to. That's it.'

'The town must be busier in the summer, with holidaymakers?'

'Bit livelier.'

'Where would you like to live?'

Cheryl turned to her and frowned. 'I int moving. I go up my Mum's and dump Troy on her if I want to have a good time.' She tossed her braids back. 'It's convenient.' She pulled Troy's dummy out and thrust it in her pocket. The child never stirred. 'Where d'you come from?'

'London. Excuse me,' Eve smiled, got up and went to talk to Hester who refilled glasses without stopping. Already Eve's ability to focus and concentrate was failing.

'Do you have any more family, apart from your daughter?' Hester asked.

Eve pretended not to hear and downed her third glassful. But Hester just repeated herself.

'No,' Eve mumbled and crossed the room again.

Another strange old couple with matching thatches of swept-back thick white hair looked up and raised their glasses to her. She grinned back.

'Hi, gorgeous.' Choker stared down his scimitar nose. 'Come and sit here and tell me all about yourself.'

Eve, unwilling to be questioned, shook her head, made her apologies to Hester and left at the same time as the Tomblings. She carefully negotiated the stairs, clutching the banisters.

In her flat she drank a half a litre of water and crept to bed.

A motorbike raced up the hill past the house with an ugly howl. Then silence again.

Below, through the floorboards, she could hear the feminine tones of Amos. She couldn't make out his words, but he sounded excited, then angry. He must be on the phone, she thought, there was no response to his monologue. Eventually he appeared to be sobbing. Then there was quiet again. She was uneasy.

Thinking of Jez, she remembered how adventurous she was as a little girl, how she ran ahead through forests, or sand dunes, or winding lanes. She visualised those small legs trotting in front of her. At last, she drifted off to sleep.

When she woke, the pain in her skull was powerful. Serve me right, she thought, no one forced me to drink so much.

Light streamed through a gap in the curtains. Gulls called above. She stood carefully and went to walk on the beach until she felt better. Shipden meant reassurance, she decided, it had something to do with the same salty smell of seaside holidays.

Back in the flat she decided to spend the day painting her bathroom yellow and white. She turned on her portable radio and balanced it against the basin, but was thinking about Jez and not really listening to Radio Four until a familiar voice with a slight foreign accent caught her attention. It was a recording of Choker, reviewing a young man's first collection of poems. He damned with the faintest possible praise and read a sonnet in a loud, sarcastic tone. This so annoyed Eve that she turned the radio off. Then, minutes later, she put it on again as she remembered she wanted to hear his full name. It was too late, the programme had ended.

She was on her knees working on the skirting board when she heard a presenter say, 'Two hundred and ten thousand people are reported missing every year in this country. One in three are never seen again.' She imagined the poor relatives waiting in fear for news. And those lost young girls disappearing without trace.

She put down her brush, changed her clothes and went out again.

Walking through the town she came across a little Viennese style café, its windows steamed up against the cool air.

Inside it was warm and full of the aroma of chocolate and coffee. The thick floral carpet, well-upholstered banquette seats, blue and white wall tiles and faint violin waltz music appealed. Not only were there framed posters of plates of pastries and cream-laden cakes, but also what looked like the real thing in a revolving display cabinet. She liked the slow ceiling fans, sluggishly stirring the warm air, she admired the carved cuckoo clock which told the wrong time, and she especially liked the girl waitresses in their lace-trimmed dirndl skirts.

From her corner table she watched as elderly ladies in pleated skirts and cardigans pressed invisible cake crumbs to their lips and stirred sugar with tinkling spoons in china cups. Two wore the sort of hats that were fashionable fifty years earlier.

Middle-aged coast walkers in solid boots and thick pullovers chomped more substantial food. Their faces shone, weather-beaten and enthusiastic, their eyes gleamed above steaming fish pies.

With eyes hidden behind narrow dark glasses, two young men in worn black leather drank wine and consulted bits of paper pulled from wallets. They spoke an Eastern European language unfamiliar to Eve.

Like Cheryl, the waitresses were barelegged. It must be a Norfolk thing, she thought, after a while a girl's mottled, naked legs must become weathered and impervious to the blasting cold wind.

Relaxed, she drank her coffee. It felt good to be looked after, to have attention from someone; she was very conscious of being alone. There was nobody to notice what she did here, in Shipden, nobody to care.

'Everything all right?' The waitress in the short-sleeved white blouse grinned at her as she swept crumbs from the next table. Her hands and arms were soft and pale.

As Eve nodded, her mobile rang loudly. It seemed incongruous there. An offensive noise issuing from inside her bag. She'd neither realised it was switched on, nor intended it to be. People turned to stare. Was this an emergency?

'Hello,' she said, cautiously.

'Is that you, Eve? I'm just back from a tour in the States. I must talk to you. Where are you?' The voice was low and urgent.

'Leo. I can't speak now. Ring me later.' As she snapped the phone off, her hand trembled.

She paid the bill and went out into the hostile wind again. Making straight for the sea front she stopped at the first litterbin, half full of greasy chip papers. She pulled her phone from her bag and chucked it straight in. It fell with a clatter to lie unseen under the rubbish. She walked away.

That's it, she thought. I don't ever have to speak to Leo

again. I don't need a mobile phone. The few people I want to talk to have my new phone number at the flat. I don't need to think about Leo.

But she couldn't help it.

She'd known him for a long time. He worked as an actor, but more often was 'resting' or in a series of temporary jobs, sometimes as a film extra. In the past few years, he'd earned substantial sums at an escort agency. He was her age, late thirties, and very conscious of his attractiveness and the relentless dance of time leaving its, so far, slight marks on his appearance. 'That Leo's a vain bloke,' said Eve's friends, laughing at him.

'My face is my fortune,' he always said, 'and my body. I must be desirable if I'm going to break into films.' But his big breaks were slow in coming and he spent a lot of time scrounging from his friends, Eve included.

She managed to put him to the back of her mind, then recalled her phone.

What if someone found and used it? The cost to her account might be horrendous. And the mobile had been expensive enough in the first place. And her personal information, new work number and contacts were on it. What was she doing, throwing it away? She should bin Leo, not her phone.

She ran back and retrieved it.

At home she logged on to see if Jez had emailed.

Mum, I'm in Melaka now and really enjoying it. Everything's cheap, it only cost me £4 to travel on the bus from Singapore and the bus fare to Kuala Lumpur is £1.50 or thereabouts. I'll go in a day or two. I'm in a very basic hotel, really cheap but ten times better than a backpackers' hostel with crappy old mixed sex dorms and putrid showers. I got sick of those in Australia and New Zealand. I'm very happy and putting on tons of weight, ballooning into a huge bloaty whale person eating too many noodles and doughy pratas. In one of the Malaysian food halls today I decided on a seafood stall and chose my mysterious and suspicious bits of fish, and the lady cooked them for me in a laksa noodle dish, quite spicy. I always eat with the locals and have grown used to eating with chopsticks now. Must go, my eardrums are on the verge of exploding. I'm in a noisy cybercafé full of Malaysian kids playing a loud internet game that involves screaming and blasts going off and booms and explosions and every now and then they all leap up and run around and swap computers for some odd reason. Lots of love Bloaty Noodle Eater xxx

Jez. Glad you're eating well. You must look after yourself. I'm having a great time, settling in. There are a couple of young people your age living in this house, so it's quite lively. I'm trying to sort myself out ready to start teaching. Reading my old textbooks is making me anxious. But I'll be fine. You know me. I'll be on top of things in no time. And it'll be fun going on the train, much better than being stuck in the tube under the earth. This is a healthy life. Miss you. Love M.

She thought again about Leo. Thankfully he didn't know where she was. She'd keep her mobile off. She didn't want his calls and texts. Why couldn't people just leave her alone?

April

Easter had been and gone. The weather improved. Weeks earlier, Eve had filled in her CRB application form and been cleared to work with children and youngsters. She became used to her new job.

The students were agreeable and keen, the other staff polite, though distant. So many of the staff were part-timers too, there were few opportunities to become friendly. Every time she went to the college, she met different people. One day at coffee time she sat, unknowingly, in a chair reserved for the head of some obscure department.

'That's mine,' said the slight man with narrowed eyes. Without a word she picked up her books and left the cold room.

There was more paperwork than she'd expected. Although she only travelled to the city two days a week, she still spent another day at home on preparation and form-filling. She planned to take her students on visits to art galleries. There was a great deal to keep her occupied.

She enjoyed the trips by small train rat-a-tatting its way through the flat meadows covered in new green shoots. Hawthorn hedges starred with white, and yellow gorse bloomed beside the track. In gardens, clouds of lilac and cherry blossom floated in front of houses. Pheasants strutted on ploughed fields and through drifts of bluebells in woods. She'd never seen so many ancient churches at once. They stood, round and square-towered, as they'd stood for centuries, defensive and dominant, isolated and unchanging in the countryside under a huge sky.

As her evening train approached Shipden she always looked out to the left for the white windmill near the sea where Hester told her Walter de la Mare had once lived.

Finding any connections to the past pleased her. One day

Hester stood at one of Eve's high windows and told her how the town had attracted writers, artists and wealthy people a hundred years ago.

'They stayed in the Grand Hotel and nearby,' she said, pointing. 'Look, see the big mock Tudor house there. That was the first house to be built in the avenue. It was owned by the Maharajah of Cooch Behar and he often invited the Prince of Wales to stay. You can imagine the discreet goings-on at night. Great place for mistresses here.' She laughed salaciously. 'Other summer visitors were Oscar Wilde, Alfred Lord Tennyson, even Winston Churchill. It was after the railways came and Clement Scott made Poppyland fashionable.' She came away from the window. 'It's not so chic now. But that's what I like, this part, its shabby gentility.'

After she'd gone, Eve stood at her different windows until the sky darkened, just watching the traffic and people on the streets. The men and women walked in different ways: slowly, carrying loads with heads bowed, or sprightly and erect like Lowry's matchstick men. The children bobbed, hopping on the pavement. She watched the restaurant lights come on, the fluorescent blue of the working kitchen and the warm orange of the room where customers sat. Shop lights went out and house windows lit up.

She could see the strings of coloured illuminations hanging above the cliffs, and far away on the sea the tiny lights of ships moving across the darkness. High above pinpricks of stars glittered.

Seeing Cheryl walk away down the street past the wall of knapped flints, Eve thought of Jez. She wondered how the childhood experiences of the two girls, born around the same time, had differed. How had Cheryl been brought up?

Eve felt like a spy, a watcher who wasn't involved with other people's lives, just someone who was waiting, alone, for something that might never happen.

She left the window and went to her computer.

Mum, I liked Melaka and stayed in a guesthouse run by a nice Mr Tan. He was very helpful and loaned me 20 ringgits. I'm always disorganised with my currency. Health and safety is a nightmare. I was just having a shower and saw it was an electric one plugged into a socket above my head. It's easy to get electrocuted here. And I watched some men putting up "scaffolding" in Singapore. They climbed thin rods, tied them, pulled up more rods, tied them, clambering right up the side of a huge skyscraper. Made me shudder. Kuala Lumpur was big and smelly and full of people rushing around and pushing food carts about. Went up the tower, you can see for miles. Yesterday I flew to Bangkok and I'm in a hostel now. There are hawkers' food stalls everywhere and they have chickens hanging up, the smell is awesome. Some of the food is mysterious but the fruit is great. Don't fancy the fish as the rivers and canals here are thick and green and sludgy, but I'm eating lots of noodles. The traffic is phenomenal, I used a tuk tuk today (one of those 3 wheeled motorbike things). I talked to someone who said that they are keen for people to teach English here in Thailand and in Korea and China. I may give it a go. It would be useful experience. Lots of love Jez.

Jez. Noodles are good. I had durian once, very strange fruit, smelled like drains. Here in Shipden, crabs are the thing, they're delicious. I just love them. The best dish in the world, though, is fresh lobster. I could live on bananas and lobsters, if I could afford it. I've been putting photos of you all over the flat. Not just the big school one, but some of your baby and toddler ones. You were so sweet. Do you remember your white snowsuit with the rabbit ears? We were both so sad when you couldn't squeeze into it any more. Eat well, take care of yourself and have a great time. I miss you. Love M.

Eve, sleepless and lonely, imagined Jez teaching for years in some faraway school beyond the mountains of Korea.

She lay still watching the hand move almost imperceptibly around her bedside clock face.

At ten past one she heard a door creak on the floor below. Then someone climbed the stairs, slowly and deliberately. The familiar wheezing meant it was Amos.

She wondered what he could be up to, and pulled her duvet higher.

On the landing he stood, gasping for breath outside her door.

She waited, not making a sound, forcing herself to lie immobile as the minutes passed. Recalling the chain on her door was a reassurance. No one could get into her flat.

His breathing became less laboured, but still he stood outside.

Her anxiety turned to anger. What was the matter with the man? What was he doing? She crept out of bed. It was dark but a strip of landing light shone under her door, partially blocked by Amos's shoes.

Then down below the main door opened and someone ran up the flights of stairs. It must be Darren. Amos snorted and began his heavy descent.

She could hear Darren's low voice. 'Awright?'

Amos only grunted and continued his slow progress. By the time he reached his own flat, Darren was already running his bath water.

Eve listened to the gushing. She'd heard that a few times through the wall if she happened to be awake around 2am. She grimaced at the strangeness of certain men, then stopped being concerned and slipped back into bed.

Days passed. The missing girl had still not been found. Then a body was discovered floating in a river near her home and the media gave it a great deal of attention. It was confirmed as the body of an old woman who had disappeared months back. Newspapers and television ran stories that the missing youngster was probably with a secret boyfriend. Other incidents hit the headlines and there was no more speculation about the girl.

Eve kept busy, thinking about bodies and sunlight falling on water.

Mum. I went to Chiang Mai and didn't know they were celebrating Thai New Year, the festival of Songkran or Water festival. Every time I stepped out in the street I was drenched. All the locals hang around with water pistols and buckets of the stuff and soak each other. It was a bit of a giggle at first, especially as it was so hot, but when you're walking along and a pick-up truck drives past and the locals hang off the back and throw icy cold buckets of water at you it does get irritating. Still, I represented England very well and didn't curse, but smiled and giggled as yet another small child shot the contents of his pistol down my back. Have seen some enticing menus—'Fried catfish with tasty ingredients', and 'Chiangmai sausage in hot and sour taste'… but am eating large amounts of fried noodles. They love karaoke here, especially the Elvis impersonators who all have problems pronouncing 'sh' and refer to 'fools russing in' all the time. I'm on the island of Phuket now, which is full of fat Norwegian men who walk around with their beer bellies hanging out. They are all covered in big tattoos and have little Thai ladies with them. I'm going back to Bangkok. Big kisses from Thai shrimp soup eater.

Jez. Don't you russ into anything. Do you remember the beer bellies we saw in Margate? You were quite little and asked me if those daddies were going to have babies. I'm glad men can't have infants, it's such a special woman thing. Looking back, I think my happiest time was when I was pregnant with you, feeling you grow inside me. And then when you were born, I had the most overpowering feeling of joy. The bond between mother and child is the strongest in the world. Man and woman love may alter over time, but not maternal love. Enough of this, I'm getting quite emotional. My love always, M.

One evening Eve was eating macaroni cheese for her solitary supper when the phone rang. An unusual occurrence.

'Hi. Eve? This is Choker here.'

'How do you know my number?'

'That's not very friendly, sweetheart. Hope you don't mind. I saw it in Hester's book the other day. Look, can you come and have a drink with me, now, at The Dragon Hotel? It'll only take you a couple of minutes to get there.'

'It's a bit short notice.' Her tone was guarded. Did she really want to see him?

'Go on. I'll explain when I see you. It's to do with Hester.'

'Give me ten minutes. And I can't stay long, I've a million things to do tonight.'

'Don't tell me. Washing your hair?' The phone went dead.

Patronising git, she thought. When he looks at me his eyes seem to bore right inside my head, as if he knows what I'm thinking. And what I'm thinking is—it's a pity he's the only halfway decent looking man round here because he's so full of his own importance. Anyway, what if someone sees us drinking together and tells Hester? They seem good friends. I don't want to go behind her back. But perhaps if it's to do with her, that's fine. I really like her and she makes me laugh with her snippets of autobiography. I don't want to hurt her and even the most cynical and hard-bitten person can be wounded. But surely Hester and Choker are friends only.

Eve finished her supper and took the trouble to change into black trousers and top, to comb out the tangles in her long hair and apply mascara.

I can't think why I'm doing this, she thought. But she paused in front of her mirror, and seeing her familiar deep-set light eyes, dissatisfied mouth, sharp chin and long neck, she fluffed out her hair.

She hadn't been in The Dragon before. The old, ornamented building reared up at the top of the cliffs. Around it wove narrow, echoing streets. Inside, the rooms were panelled with dark wood and decorated with ancient copper pots and hanging greenery. Choker was leaning over the bar, laughing with the barman and blowing a kiss at a departing waitress.

He turned and saw her in the doorway. 'Eve. At last.' He beckoned. 'What are you drinking? Have a brandy.' Without waiting, he ordered the drink and when it was poured, picked up his glass and hers as well as a large, brown paper package, and led her to an out-of-the-way corner table.

'I'd like you to do me a favour. I know you're talented in the art line. Just take a look at this, will you? It's something I bought at an auction today.' He pulled the paper off a painting of a Victorian interior.

Eve tilted it to catch the light. 'This is no masterpiece, I'm afraid. I hope you didn't pay a lot. It's done by an amateur. The faces are rather crudely painted. But it's not bad.'

He laughed. 'I know that. But I had an idea about it.'

They studied the depiction of two young men in evening dress: one sitting on a chaise-longue, the other leaning against it. The long-haired, side-whiskered dandies were shown in dark dress coats and narrow breeches with straps under the insteps, white waistcoats, shirts and cravats swathed round their necks with bow ties. One held a pale handkerchief in his white-gloved hand, the other a cigarette. Shades of green drapery and yellow roses on a table made up the background.

She scrutinised the picture. 'I can't see a signature anywhere. And there's no date either.' She turned it over. On the back letters in faded ink spelled out *The Conversazione*.

'I'd like you to paint over it for me. It's to be a present for Hester. Could you replace the men's faces with her labradors' heads?'

Taken aback, she thought. 'I'm not sure that I'm very good at animals.'

'No problem. I've a photo here of them.' He took out of his pocket a large coloured snap of the dogs taken in close up on the beach.

'That's fine. I could manage that.' She wondered if she would be paid for her work, but money wasn't mentioned. He doesn't realise how valuable my time is, she thought, or how very useful a cheque would be.

He pointed out the differences between the dogs, the details Hester knew so well. 'She'll really be over the moon if you do this. You know just how much she dotes on those dogs. She'll hang it over the fireplace and we'll both be in favour.' He glanced at her glass. 'The other half?'

She shook her head.

He continued. 'Not that I'm not in favour right now, mind you. But it's coming up to the anniversary of Hugo's death and I want to take her mind off that.'

She noticed that his face and hands gleamed darkly. His olive skin seemed most un-Norfolk. Briefly imagining him without his clothes, she couldn't stop herself blushing. 'I must go. Did you know Hugo?'

He stood. 'Yes. A prize shit. Led her a dance. But you know what it's like, we all remember the good bits of a relationship.' He bent, stroked the hair from her face and kissed her cheek. 'I'll leave this with you. Can you do it in the next couple of weeks? I'll get back to you. I've a deadline for a series of reviews and critical articles so I'll be out of circulation for a bit.' He gave off vitality like electricity. 'Thanks a million. You're a real sweetie.'

She lugged the heavy thing back and up the flights of steps. Cheryl was having a party and the noise of loud music, young men shouting and Troy crying came from her flat. Eve allowed herself a moment's sympathy for the Tomblings below, then shut her door against the racket drifting up the stairs.

Dumping the painting in a corner, she settled in front of her computer.

Mum. Was up at 5am today to catch the bus to the Thai/ Cambodia border. After a while I noticed we were on the wrong side of the road and the driver was having a little kip. Spent the rest of the journey watching his every movement and ensuring his eyes were open. At the border had a great hassle with the next driver as he'd sold my prepaid ticket to someone else. Finally managed to squeeze with other people into a rickety old car. We ricocheted our way 198 km to Siem Reap on a dirt track full of pot holes and rocks, taking nightmare hours. We only had 2 stops— just long enough for the driver to relieve himself long and loud right next to the car. Was tempted to go behind a bush, but you can't because of the unexploded landmines. They are a massive problem here, and there are loads of people with missing limbs. I have heard from backpackers that many tourists here are held up at gunpoint.
Lots of love from Sweaty Jez.

Jez. Please do take care. I'm very concerned about you. You mustn't take risks. It's not worth it. Your safety means everything to me. It's better to spend all your money on reliable transport than put yourself in danger. Still, I mustn't nag, you're not seven. Though that was a lovely age, you wanted to be a ballet dancer, remember? That tiny, frilly, pink tutu from Mrs Verger turned up in one of my boxes the other day. I hung it in the back garden to get the mildew out. It was your favourite garment once and Father Christmas called you his Sugar Plum Fairy before you spilled your orange juice down his front. I look forward to your next message. Hugs. M.

The noise from Cheryl's flat increased. Every few minutes someone outside at the front would shout up to her window.

Eve looked out from on high and saw two shaven-headed youngsters with a dog on a string waiting impatiently. She heard Hester's dogs bark in warning and Vernon Tombling banging on Cheryl's door. 'Turn it down!' he shouted. 'Think of other people.'

There was no noticeable effect. Eve prepared for a long night. She put her headphones on to listen to her choice of music, Dave Brubeck, and applied emulsion on top of the pale faces on Choker's canvas.

Hours later she took her headphones off, cleared her paint mess and fell into bed. A rhythmical thump, thump, still audible, meant Cheryl hadn't finished the night.

On the point of sleep, seeing dim faces crowding into her dream space, Eve was jolted into consciousness by a battering on her door. The heavy knocker slammed down and fists thundered against the wood. 'Bitch!' Slurred speech and drunken laughter indicated several young men on the landing.

Wide awake, Eve sat up. I'm not going to open the door, she thought. If they go on doing that, I'll call the police.

But the door bashing stopped as abruptly as it began, footsteps thudded downstairs and the front door crashed closed. The shouting and swearing faded down the street.

May

The weather was blustery and wet. Cheryl, in bad odour with everyone else at Strand House, kept a low profile. Her curtains were always closed until noon anyway and Troy could be seen in the mornings at the window behind the drapery, staring silently down at the street. Eventually, a child's video would be heard and the curtains drawn back. Very occasionally Cheryl would go out with Troy in his buggy in the afternoon, but the evening was the time she normally took him out. Eve saw them hanging outside different pubs, Cheryl statuesque with a cigarette, asking for a light or talking to tattooed men, while Troy gazed into space, cut off from communication by his dummy.

One brighter morning Eve wanted chrome plated hooks to fix to the back of her kitchen and bathroom doors, so made her way along the narrow pavements to the nearest ironmonger's.

As she stepped over the threshold, she saw Amos Postle solidly behind the wide, mahogany counter. As he appeared to be her height, she assumed he stood on something out of view. He wore a gigantic brown overall with a row of green biros lined in the upper pocket. His short, pallid fingers, like raw chipolatas, poked over the back edge of the counter. His mouth hung open as he chewed something. At that moment he turned his spherical head and caught sight of her. His eyes registered alarm. He flushed a deep beet colour and, pulling a huge handkerchief from a lower pocket, began an exhaustive nose-blowing.

'I didn't know you worked here.' She smiled at him.

Without a word, he beckoned to the only other person in the shop, a teenaged salesgirl occupied with a magazine, and indicated that she should serve Eve. Then he ponderously stepped down from the box or shelf on which he stood and shuffled off through a door marked 'Exit. Staff only.'

Eve bought her hooks and screws, plus some kettle descaler, from the blank faced girl. 'Is Mr Postle all right?'

'Nutter,' was all the response she received. The girl went back to her magazine.

Outside sunlight cascaded from a cloudless sky. Eve walked past the neat beds of wallflowers and into the church. She'd been waiting for a good day to climb the tower, the tallest in Norfolk. It was a long, twisting way up the stone spiral to the top. One hundred and sixty feet, she remembered reading.

At the top, standing on the roof next to the wall, she caught her breath and waited for her heart to calm.

On one side the crinkled sea swept to the horizon, dotted with a few small sailing boats and distant barges. Nearer, among the white filigree wave edges, moved specks of surfing boys in wet suits. The town lay before her, its narrow, crooked streets and tumbling roofs and chimneys dwarfed. Tiny, hidden gardens splashed colour between the houses with yellow laburnum and clumps of purple flowers. Traffic moved slowly, figures were insects on the grass and beach, and beyond wooded slopes the lighthouse flashed its unending signals to the passing world.

A faraway motorbike growled down the hill, wound its way through the town and out the other side. She wondered if that could be Choker. She'd finished his dog portraits, which had taken longer than expected, fiddling with a tiny brush, taking infinite pains to differentiate the animals. The results were better than anticipated and she hoped for some appreciation.

Directly below the church, Hester crossed the road. Eve recognised the long, dark skirt, black hat hiding the face and wicker basket held on one arm. Two Labradors pulled on the leash. Hester, a small moving blot, tied them up outside the bank and went inside.

That night was warm. Eve opened her windows and stared out of each before restlessly padding around her flat. She watched the sky turn from pale green to navy, she marked a couple of essays on Surrealism, without concentrating on what she was doing, then opened a bottle of wine. Drinking on my own is so boring, she thought, remembering past evenings spent with friends in London, the hilarity and the release of emotion. She walked back and forth tensely. The wine tasted bland and dull.

Sweat slid under her arms as she identified her problem. It was desire. It had been so long since she'd been intimate with a man. She needed to be close to someone.

'Want must be my master,' she spoke aloud and wondered where that saying came from and what it meant. She remembered one of her lovers, a dominating older man who had been part of her life years earlier, an ugly Magus whom she'd adored at the time. She didn't miss him, but the affair had its sexual excitements and she ached for those again.

She thought of the recent hoarse, aroused voices of the youngsters at her door. But very young men didn't interest her with their banal conversation and inexperience and uncertainties. Perhaps she only found confidence and arrogance attractive.

In that room there was no one to touch and caress her, to hold her tightly, to say all those things she needed to hear. She wanted to be wanted. She certainly wanted. She was conscious of nothing else.

Abruptly she left the flat, keys jingling in her pocket. She ran down the stairs and out into the street. It was late, people were going home from pubs.

As she neared The Dragon Hotel, she saw Choker leaving, the yellow light behind him, the top of a bottle sticking out of his jacket pocket. A turbulence in her throat made her realise she knew what she wanted after all. Who she wanted. The reason she'd come in that direction. The tall man with the broad shoulders and the handsome profile had her hunting him down like some dizzy adolescent.

Catching up with him, she put a hand on his arm.

He turned. 'Eve. Great to see you. Are you going in my direction?'

'No. But would you like to come my way?' She stared intently at him.

He grinned and changed course. 'Let's go along here, up by the cliffs. It's a fine night, we can do some stargazing.' He laughed.

In silence they walked together up the winding path away from town. Below them to the left the sea lashed its waves against the stones in the darkness. Ahead the lighthouse swept its beams insistently every few seconds. When they came to a seat halfway up the hill, he guided her to it.

'Are you okay?' He put his arm around her.

'I'm fine. I suddenly felt lonely. It doesn't often happen to me. But I'm glad to see you.'

He leaned down and kissed her. She responded. His stubble rustled against her skin. Together they shared his whisky and kissed with increasing urgency.

'Let's have a contest. Run to the top,' he said.

They ran and ran until her heart pounded and her breath came in gasps. She couldn't keep up with him and stopped, bent double to recover. Then they went more slowly to the top of the cliffs where there were only trees and grass and rustling shrubs.

'I bet this is where the junkies come to shoot up,' she said.

'No. Not here. There is a heroin problem in the town, but they don't come as far as this.'

'How far are we going?'

'This is far enough for all the way.' He pulled her down among whispering leaves and a scent of crushed grass.

Afterwards they rolled on their backs and looked at the stars. The night air felt cool on their nakedness. He stroked her with a warm hand. 'You're an affectionate creature.'

She didn't want to say anything. Felt calm, the torrent of passion over. Pulling her clothes on again she thought, I feel so good now but hope I don't regret this, hope he doesn't feel he must send me flowers and all that sort of stuff, hope it's not going to complicate things. I needed him to take charge then, to use contraception without mentioning it, to make love to me so skilfully, without words.

He dressed, yawned and pushed the empty whisky bottle down a rabbit hole.

As they came slowly down the hill, she made an effort to talk to him about Hester's painting, but she staggered slightly and her words slurred and she found herself relieved to say goodbye at the corner where the streetlights began. He didn't suggest walking back to Strand House with her which was fine, she didn't want that anyway.

There she had difficulty getting the right key in the lock, and carefully climbing the stairs she came across the door marked 'A.Postle' ajar and Amos himself breathing heavily behind it.

'Goo'night,' she mumbled to him. But the door closed sharply.

In her bedroom she discovered her trousers all covered in grass stains and her shirt on inside out, which made her giggle.

Mum, Went in a tuk tuk to visit loads of temples, including the main Angkor Wat which is in good condition. Absolutely incredible. The temples cover an area of about 75 square km and I travelled through Cambodian villages where everyone lives in wooden shacks on stilts to keep away from the monsoon floods. Cattle wander all over the road and as soon as you stop anywhere children rush out to touch you and try to sell you little things. Spent

9 hours on a rickety old bus hurtling and ricocheting our way to Phnom Penh. Everyone deals in Thai baht, Cambodian riel and American dollars, so paying for things can be confusing. A group of us went to the Killing Fields yesterday, which was awful and we all came back in a state of shock and felt quite humbled by the whole experience. I'm going to a museum this afternoon to find out more about Cambodia. It's very hot and sweaty here. Am off to Saigon tomorrow on the bus which will take all day.
Lots of love from the perspiring traveller.

Jez. I'm full of admiration. You are really getting around. Amazing. I print out all your emails to keep and reread. There's not much to report from this end. I'm meeting more people so loneliness isn't a problem. Work's okay. The students are quite keen so the teaching keeps me busy with research. There's not much time for my own painting. I intended to start an undersea fantasy mural in the bathroom here, but I'll have to keep that idea for the future. It's bright yellow at the moment, a bit dazzling when you're sitting in the bath and the sun's shining in. A buttercup experience. Much love, M.

It was the next day. Eve put Jez's email in her special folder.

As she turned off the computer, someone knocked on her door.

Hester stood in a long purple skirt and black satin blouse.

Eve fought a pang of guilt about Choker and forced herself to appear normal. 'Hi.'

'I'm going to a plant sale to get stuff for the garden. It's for a children's charity. Want to come? I remembered it's not a work day for you.'

They drove a few miles inland to a manor house in well-tended gardens. While Hester went round the trestle tables putting her chosen plants in cardboard boxes, Eve picked out a few potted scarlet geraniums for her kitchen windowsill.

As she reached for a particularly fine specimen, a plump

arm and hand pushed Eve aside and swiftly picked the plant up. 'Mine, I think.' A rasping, yet cultured sound.

The middle-aged woman had a round plump face like a pink, shiny cushion, a button nose and fierce slit of a cashbox mouth. Her hair swung in a glossy, high-maintenance bob. Hers was the voice of authority, her gold regalia the insignia of someone in charge.

'Be my guest.' Eve laughed.

The woman looked away and, seeing Hester approach, nodded distantly to the older woman then moved her bulk on solid legs.

After Eve paid for her geraniums, she asked Hester, 'Do you know her?'

'Yes.'

They stowed the plants in the back of the car and climbed in. 'She doesn't approve of me, I'm afraid. That's Venetia Chakour. Choker's tedious wife.'

Eve coughed, taken aback. 'I didn't know he was married.'

'He doesn't act as though he is. They've always done their separate things. The irony is that she once wanted to be our local marriage guidance counsellor, but didn't want to do the training.' Hester laughed long and loud, nearly driving the old car into the side of the wrought iron gates. 'I think they call it *Relate* now.' She sniffed. 'Anyway, he never had any money and she inherited loads so he married her knowing he wouldn't have to endure a boring nine to five job. She's older than him. She doesn't like me because I knew Choker twenty years ago, long before she met him. Just a handsome boy he was. That amazing nose. Those well-defined bones,' she mused. 'I was in my prime.' She smirked reflectively. 'He's written some lovely lines about me.' The car bumped along the lane for a while. 'We stayed friends and now he comes around to help with my writing about Hugo. Venetia hates that. She keeps away from me. We move in different circles. She's tremendously pious and priggish, likes to do good

works and let everyone know about it. You know the sort.'
After a while she added, 'Venetia means blessed. Blessed
Venetia.' She guffawed.

'Chakour doesn't sound English.'

'No. His parents were Lebanese or Egyptian. French
influence, too, I believe. They died and he was sent to
boarding school in the West Country when he was five.
Some family connection. The boys didn't pronounce his
name properly. They called him "Choker" and it stuck.
Nobody uses his first name, Marc. French spelling.'

'Marc Chakour,' she tried it out. 'It doesn't sound like him
at all.' She studied the banks of cow parsley as they swished
by in the car. 'Where do they live?'

'The place that belonged to her parents. It's a Georgian
house south of the town. They rattle around there.'

'No children?'

'No. Just as well.'

*Mum. Travelling round Phnom Penh was hair-raising. The
cheapest way is to hop on the back of a mo-ped and give yourself
up to the terrors of the road. I just rammed my hat down over my
eyes and clenched my mouth to stop myself screaming out. The
traffic comes from every direction with honking horns and no one
slows at junctions. Caught a bus over the border into Vietnam,
took about nine hours but the roads aren't so potholed. Am in
Saigon now and the people are really friendly. Went to the Cu Chi
tunnels which were used by the Viet Cong. They lived and worked
down there. You know I hate small spaces and forced myself in.
Couldn't get back as there were a lot of impatient blokes behind
me, so I blasted along the tunnel at about 100 miles an hour and
burst out at the first exit point like a hysterical rabbit chased by a
ferret. Went to the War Remnants Museum, which was ghastly
and harrowing, especially the preserving jars containing
malformed bodies of babies showing the effects of Agent Orange.
I've been on a cyclo, one of those rickshaw things where you sit in*

the chair in front while the driver pedals you on the bicycle bit at the back. It's a hoot as you are pushed into the traffic and have to watch as everything hurtles towards you. I'm getting used to it and no longer scream and get off feeling all white and trembly. You can buy anything to eat in the animal line here, dog and pickled snakes in jars. I stick to the vegetable noodle soup. Miss you. Lots of love Jez xxx

Jez. So you're not a carnivore yet? Sticking to the veg. sounds fine. I eat crab in different ways, my special chowder, in omelettes or puff pastry, all excellent. Not that I do much cooking for myself. I'm getting lazy about that and it's boring fiddling in the kitchen for just one person. Hester downstairs is a laugh and I sometimes invite her for something to eat because she cheers me up. She's my surrogate mother. She mothers all the people living in this house and is especially patient with Cheryl who can be thoughtless and annoying. Not like you. I miss you. Love M.

All the time in the recesses of Eve's mind lurked thoughts about Jez, journeying on without her. She had nightmares about accidents and abductions and woke at night fighting to calm herself.

She often compared Jez to Cheryl. The Norfolk girl has that same soft and shiny complexion, long legs, and confidence, thought Eve, leaning over her windowsill to water her geraniums.

She watched as below, Darren, a thin, agitated spider, pushed tiny Troy on his little bike on the tarmac.

Darren glanced up and saw her. He shouted, 'Can you do me a favour? Cheryl's not back. She dumped Troy on me and promised to be home an hour ago.' He pulled a grimace. 'I've to go out.' He seemed extra twitchy. 'Can you look after him?'

'Yes,' she shouted back. 'Bring him up to me and leave a note for Cheryl so she'll know where he is.'

Eve took care of the child for the rest of the day. Holding

her hand, he walked to the beach, which seemed unfamiliar to him. He played happily in the sand, ate an ice cream messily and watched the waves with amazement.

She remembered caring for tiny Jez, and felt touched by the way little children trusted her.

Back in Strand House, Eve knocked on Cheryl's door, which was ajar. No one came and she pushed it open to search for disposable nappies. The flat was a tip with broken plastic cars and partially eaten takeaways strewn about, the curtains closed and a television left on. She turned the noise off and changed Troy's nappy. He accepted everything she did without protest. As she talked to him and smiled, he just stared up at her and said nothing.

In her own flat they shared her supper of pasta and yoghourt, played games of 'peep-bo', during which he became animated and boisterous, running to hide, time and time again, behind the chairs, then they once again returned to Cheryl's place. There, Eve bathed him, found him pyjamas, gave him a bottle of milk and put him into his cot. He lay, apparently unconcerned, clutching a spotted giraffe, rolling his eyes sleepily and sucking his bottle.

Eve found a telephone book by the sink. She searched through and under 'Mum' saw six different local numbers crossed out. The last number appeared to be viable. She tried it.

Someone answered. 'Hello.'

'Is that Cheryl's mother?'

'Who wants to know?'

'This is Eve Key. I'm a neighbour of Cheryl's at Strand House. I wondered if she was with you. I've been looking after Troy for her.'

'Sod it. She ain't gone off again!'

'I don't know where she is. Do you have any idea?'

'That bitch Cheryl. She do this to me all the time. I'll come and get the little bugger.' The phone slammed.

After half an hour, a bony, anxious woman about Eve's age pushed open Cheryl's door. 'I hint got the key. That's why she don't lock it. Someone left the front door open.' She fingered back her tangled fuzz of brittle bleached hair and lit a cigarette. Her worried eyes narrowed. Without another word she lifted her sleeping grandson out of his cot and into his buggy, tucked a knitted blanket round him, bumped him down the stairs and trundled him off into the night.

Eve pulled Cheryl's door to and climbed the stairs, troubled about the child.

June

Mum. I'm in Hanoi now. Had a good flight. A very kind nice lovely lady at the check in desk gave me a first class seat! I'd asked for one with leg room and was the tallest in the check-in queue by two feet, so she probably thought it was best to pop me in first class to keep my legs out of the way and stop people falling over me. I'm staying in the old quarter, which is crammed with little lanes, shops and cafes. There are lots of women carrying huge baskets of fruit and vegetables, struggling under great weights, while the men sit on their mo-peds waiting for people who want lifts. I went to visit Ho Chi Minh who is embalmed in a mausoleum, but by the time I'd found him, at 10.30am, it was closing time! Spent the rest of the day visiting museums. Everyone is really friendly. Lots of love Jez xxx

Jez. Glad you are enjoying Hanoi. I have a Vietnamese student in one of my classes. She works harder than anyone else and her English is excellent for someone who's only been here a short time. We had a snack together in the college canteen yesterday and she told me how much she's missing her family in the country. She's obsessed by butterflies and her paintings of them are really original, on silk and in shades of purple and lilac. I'm trying to help her get an exhibition. No chance to organise one for myself, I'm just not producing the work. However my social life is improving, I went to the theatre last week with Hester. Bit of a boring modern play, though. No laughs and lots of long, meaningful pauses. Enjoy yourself. Love, M.

Eve came downstairs carrying a plastic bowl full of wet washing to hang in the back garden. Seen from the window, a profusion of delicate poppies filled one flowerbed with a scarlet haze.

Out there she saw Vernon labouring by the hedge,

digging a large hole with a small, polished spade.

'I'm rearranging this bit, putting shrubs in here and making a rockery there,' he explained, wheezing and sweaty faced. 'Hester's dogs don't help. I wish she wouldn't let them loose here. They're forever digging things up.' He bent to his work as Eve sympathised and pegged out her clothes.

Choker had given Hester the painting the night before. Eve, invited to the downstairs flat for a drink to see her unwrap it, had been excessively praised for her skill.

'That's bloody marvellous! Unbelievably good. So like my handsome boys! Thank you both so much for such a fantastic present. I've never had such an appropriate gift before. I'm speechless.' But Hester wasn't, and didn't stop talking until Choker had hung the painting over her mantelpiece in the best position and she and the dogs admired it in a silence that lasted a whole minute.

Eve felt pleasure that her work was appreciated, but in Hester's presence she couldn't look at Choker. Her face burned as she remembered their intimacy. She felt emotional towards him and could hardly trust herself to speak.

He invited Hester to dinner and they both wanted Eve to join them.

'No, thanks very much but I can't. I've a briefcase full of essays to mark and reports that have to be done tonight,' she lied, conscious that just then she couldn't cope with being with both of them.

She ran upstairs to listen to the news on the radio.

There was no more information on the missing girl and her thoughts turned to Cheryl who still hadn't returned.

Darren said she'd promised to be straight back from the shops to pick Troy up and she hadn't taken anything with her. 'She don't usually leave him for so long. But she's always dumping him on people. Her Mum takes the kid quite often.'

Hester had rung that lady who didn't seem concerned about her daughter's welfare, only Troy's. Hester had also

46

communicated with the police.

What if something awful had happened to Cheryl, Eve wondered. But surely not in Shipden. This is such a very safe place. Nothing horrible could happen in this little town.

She put her plastic bowl away and started making coffee when the Strand House front door buzzed.

She picked up the intercom. 'Hello.'

'Guess who this is, darling heart.'

A spoon fell from her fingers. It rang harshly on the tiles. She said nothing.

'I know you're there.'

That careful enunciation caused problems with her regular breathing. She didn't want to think about him. Why couldn't he leave her alone? Leo Prior was outside the house and she couldn't pretend she didn't live here.

'I'll let you in.' She pressed the button to open the front door. 'I'm right at the top.'

He climbed the stairs and entered her flat, hugged her and flung himself on the sofa.

'How did you know where I was?' She rubbed her forehead.

He jumped up and crouched beside her. His face was sweaty and unshaven. 'There's something the matter with your phone. I couldn't reach you so I persuaded the woman who bought your flat to let me have your new address. Said I was your lost cousin. Described you truthfully as a beautiful pocket-sized blonde with pale turquoise eyes and a liking for moonstone jewellery. I gave the impression of being respectable. Even wore my suit.'

'Pocket-sized blonde. Good God! You went to a lot of trouble on my account. What do you want?' She moved to the door.

He went back to sprawl on the sofa. 'That's not nice, Eve. We're mates, remember? Go back a long time. I couldn't get through to you on the phone, so decided to come and see you in person. Have a little holiday by the sea. I borrowed Doug's car; he won't need it for a bit.' He stared nonchalantly around. 'This is minimalist. Very cool.' He turned to her. 'And how are you? Do you like living in the boondocks?'

'Very much and I'm fine thanks. The back of beyond suits me well.'

'Can I stay a few days? I'm skint since I got back. My theatrical agent's damned hopeless, no auditions coming up. But I went to my old Soho agency yesterday and I've some bookings for next week. One or two clients from last year mentioned my name.'

'That escort business?' She cringed.

'My dear, it's brilliant to be paid to be taken out. The best restaurants in London, champers, caviar, subservient waiters, I love it all.'

'And the extras?' She avoided his gaze.

'Everything has its price, you know. Though some of these middle-aged business women just want someone to listen to. I'm a good conversationalist, know how to flirt, know how to satisfy my clients. You know me. I've always had a high sex drive.' He yawned. 'I take a lot of care to give each woman something she's never had before. I make sure I'm looking good, shave my body, take my vibrators with me. I'm very professional and attentive to a woman's needs.'

Eve felt cold. 'You can't stay here, Leo.' She took an old jacket from the back of a chair and put it on.

He leaned close and she was aware of his garlic breath. He grabbed her hand. 'Go on, angel. I'll be no trouble. We were good friends, remember. Just let me stay a little while. You won't regret it.' He pulled out his wallet and took out a single five-pound note. 'Look, that's all I've got. The petrol getting here cleaned me out.' He put an arm round her shoulders.

She shrugged it off. 'You shouldn't have come. Don't think I'm going to pay for your company. I can't afford it. And I certainly don't want any extras.'

'Don't get on your high horse. Are you in a relationship right now?'

'No.'

'See. You're the same as me. You don't want emotional attachments. We don't need relationships. We can just enjoy each other's company for a bit. I'll cook for you, do the domestic stuff while you're at work, then I'll bugger off back to London and earn myself a fortune, charge a thousand pounds for a good night out, and in a while buy myself a decent car and designer clothes and treat you to a holiday in Las Vegas.'

'You must be joking.'

'Okay Greece, then.' He stood and stared out of the window. 'Tell you what, perhaps I can start my own business here.'

She giggled. 'Leo, you're bonkers. There's no one round here who wants a male escort. Shipden's full of crab fishermen and people without money, or next to none, like me. There are holidaymakers now, mostly retired folk or families with little children. Women here don't need to pay for sex.'

'What do you do for it?' he asked slyly.

'For sex? Mind your own business.'

'You haven't asked me if I'd like a drink? I'm gasping for a scotch.' Again, he went down on his knees in front of her. 'Go on. Remember Brighton? I saved you once. Be kind to me now.'

She thought of Jez. At least she's out of the way. She weakened. 'You can have a coffee and then I'll show you round town. You can stay until the weekend and sleep on my sofa bed. But don't try any funny business. I don't want you coming into my bedroom in the middle of the night. None of that. I mean it.' Her look was stern.

'We're just old friends. Okay.' He scrambled to his feet. 'Coffee it is,' he said mournfully.

After a couple of days of Leo, Eve could think of nothing but being free of him again. He never stopped talking and constantly wanted to go to pubs and restaurants, yet she had limited resources and was reluctant to spend her meagre savings on him.

'Lighten up, girl. You're a long time dead. Enjoy life, like me.' He shook his butter-coloured curls and strutted round the table, pointing his bare feet.

All the time his mobile phone kept ringing and he would turn his back to her or retire into the little bathroom and have conversations, *sotto voce*, he obviously didn't want her to hear.

'What's all this about? Who's bothering you?' She felt a small concern for him. 'Are you in trouble?'

'Nothing worse than usual. I owe a bit of money, that's all. I can sort it.' But he didn't look hopeful and spent a lot of time gnawing his knuckles and cursing under his breath. 'Don't suppose you could lend me five grand?' After one glance at her expression: 'No, thought not. Never mind.'

The one good aspect of his stay was that Amos Postle stopped coming up at night and standing silently on vigil outside Eve's door. The fat man resumed his long, emotional monologues on the phone, climaxing in audible sobs. Although Eve felt pity, it was mixed with something close to fear, and she avoided him.

On the third night, Eve's phone rang while she was reaching to lift a chicken and leek casserole from the oven.

Her guest had no hesitation answering. 'Leo here.' He put on his Olivier voice. 'Yes. This is her number. She's here... No. We're rather busy this evening. I'm staying a while with her... I'm an old friend... I could tell you all about her... '

'Leo!' she shouted, advancing on him.

'Suit yourself, ducky.' He ended on a camp Kenneth Williams tone and replaced the receiver.

'Who was that?'

'A rude foreigner who wanted to meet you for a drink. I

put him off. See how useful I am to you? A sort of guard dog. He sounded quite put out, your admirer.'

'Yes, he would be.' She smiled to herself.

The next day Leo took himself off while Eve was at work. She noticed the car was missing as she approached the house and ran up the stairs hopefully. Sure enough, a note scribbled in his huge curly writing lay on her table.

Thanks, Evey-angel, for your lovely hospitality! Must get back to the Great Wen as the prospect of Money looms. Goody! Hope to see you when I hit the greatest Big Time. Love you to bits. Leo xxx

Mm, she thought, the owner of the car probably wants it back. Anyway, thank goodness for that. I couldn't have coped a day longer.

Glancing round to check nothing was missing, she dumped her briefcase.

She realised just how much she enjoyed solitude. She liked being alone, not having to bother to cook if she didn't feel like it, able to go out on her own for a drink or something to eat, and—if she didn't have College work—reading for hours, taking long baths, painting as the mood took her. Before the advent of Leo, she was painting a series of watercolour views of Shipden, commissioned by the Grand Hotel, and was eager to get back to the well-paid work.

At once the weather turned hot and she made time to lie on the quiet beach in a bikini, acquiring a tan, ignoring advice concerning skin cancer. Hester, in particular, proud of the unblemished whiteness of her own flesh, made much of what she called Eve's 'madness'. Eve felt better, healthier, when the sun shone on her. She smoothed oils and creams on her limbs and continued soaking the heat when she could.

One of the last days of the college term, she opened her

newspaper on the train to see what she had expected for so long. The body of the missing girl had been found in a wood miles from her home.

She thought of her own Jez and, as the train rattled, offered a prayer for her safety to any deity who might be on her wavelength.

July

Mum. I have just been staying in a village on a river, a place called Hoi An where I've had a mysterious pair of wrap-around trousers made. I'm not entirely sure how to get in and out of them. Had a long bus journey in a vehicle packed with people and we roared through the night with me balanced on a pile of rucksacks. I was awake all night apart from the one hour we drove through the Demilitarized Zone, which was the one bit of the journey I wanted to be awake for—typical! Will be sorry to leave Vietnam, it's so beautiful. I shall miss the crowds piled onto one mo-ped with the baby balanced on the tank, and the ladies on mo-peds with long evening gloves and little scarves over their faces. Sat on the train from Hoi An, looking out at the fields of people picking rice, and the fabulous mountains behind, it's very picturesque. I had a hard berth (really hard) in a six-berth compartment with lots of friendly Vietnamese people who couldn't speak any English. A nice man kindly shared his hard-boiled eggs and another chap shared his pudding, a strange bright green rice thing. It was much appreciated and I felt guilty I hadn't thought of bringing anything to eat. We were given a little supper box later with odd items, so I ate the bits that looked like vegetables and hid the carnivorous-looking things under my plastic spoon. I even did the loud long slurping and belching everyone else did, and I must say it's satisfying. Scary loo on the train, which was just a big hole in the floor. Came back to find an enormous cockroach on my pillow. Stifled a scream as I didn't want to appear to be a sissy in front of my new friends, and casually flicked it on the floor. Spent the rest of the night imagining it crawling over my face. Climbed off the train at Saigon at 5.15am today and went and sat in a café until everything opened. Just had a complete hoot watching an old man doing his exercises in front of his shop. He started off swinging his arms, then did lots of marching on the spot, which completely exhausted him, so he had to sit. Then he put his feet up on a stool and did some strenuous rowing movements with his arms. Next, he stood and jumped on and off the kerb for a bit, which tired him out again, so he had to do some marching on the spot until he got his breath back. Then he balanced his chair precariously on the kerb and climbed up and dangled off a pole hanging at his back door. He dangled there with his legs hanging down for ages before jumping down and doing some more marching on the spot. I was convulsed with hysteria and kept thinking it's just the sort of thing you should be doing every morning. Lots of love, Jez xxx

Jez. You are so right. I must take more exercise. I have been swimming in the sea a few times. It's not exactly Mediterranean warmth so you can't just float, but have to thrash about healthfully. Still, it's been really hot on the beach, and the joy is that the flat is so near I can potter down in flip flops and towelling robe over my bikini and then nip back for a shower. So handy. I envy you the mountains there. As Noel Coward said, 'Very flat, Norfolk'. And the views here are mostly sky. But there is a little bump along the coast and I walked along and climbed it and felt satisfied. But not in your league. Love, M. xxx

That early July morning Eve jogged down the cliff path to the sea, past white columbine and blackberry bushes in blossom, to the sound of a skylark singing. She ran on the beach, by the sea's edge, into the bright sunlight. Silent waves broke along the shore leaving clumps of fronded seaweed like dead birds on the sand.

I'm nearly on holiday, she thought. Everything's fine. She breathed the fresh salt scent deep into her lungs.

Running up to a weathered breakwater she paused to climb over it. There was a drop on the other side which concealed the figure of a man on the empty beach. He lay on his back with his hands behind his head and stared at the cloudless sky. It was Choker.

He turned at the slight noise she made.

'Hi,' she called. 'It's only about six o'clock. I thought I'd have this place to myself.'

He sat up. 'No such luck, I'm afraid.'

'What are you doing here?'

'Creating a poem.'

'In your head?' I'm a fool, she thought. Obviously.

'Yup.'

'I suppose I'm the person from Porlock who's ruined it for you.'

He laughed. 'Essentially it's all there.' Pulling a notebook from his jeans' pocket, he scribbled something. 'I'll just get this down before I forget.'

'I'm disturbing you.'

He jumped up and caught her hand. 'No. Don't go. I've been wanting to see you. But you've had a house guest.'

'Leo's gone now.'

'Boyfriend?'

They walked over the pale sand.

'No,' she said. 'I've known him years. No romantic involvement.'

He smiled down at her. 'You're too attractive for your own good, you know. I'd like to stay in your flat.'

'But you can't.'

'That's true.'

They stopped and she studied his long fingers and clean, oval nails. 'I have to go. I'm working today and there's paperwork to do before I catch the train.'

'I'm at the university this afternoon. Have dinner with me tonight in the city and I'll bring you back on the bike.'

'I don't think so.'

'Eve, I owe you for that brilliant painting. Indulge me, like the kind and sexy woman you are.' He smiled crookedly at her and she felt a shiver of desire.

'Good. That's settled. I'll meet you at the Royal Hotel at eight then.'

So, I'm a mistress again, she thought. Well, that's fine.

As she sprinted off the sun burned even brighter.

Days later, on holiday, she was beginning to clean the front windows of her flat from the inside, when a sleek dark car purred off the road onto the Strand House tarmac.

She looked with interest at the expensive vehicle that came to a halt directly below. After a while the passenger door opened and Amos began the task of extricating himself. Then the driver slowly emerged and came round to hold the door open for him. It was Venetia, in apricot linen, with a matching velvet hairband holding her glossy dark bob back from her round face.

Amos upright, the two stood talking beside the car while Eve above, unseen, went on with her task.

'Thanks for the lift,' he said, ungraciously.

'A pleasure. Now, Mr Postle,' Venetia murmured, 'you know I'm always here to help you in my capacity as an amateur counsellor.'

'Whass that you say?' He held a hand behind one ear.

'But you must help yourself,' she increased the volume, 'with regard to brazen women. As I said before. Don't allow yourself to be snared and persuaded. Keep to the safe and narrow path and all will be well.'

'I try,' the familiar high-pitched voice responded. 'But she always tempt me, she do. Flaunt herself at me. I can't stop thinking.'

'You must do your best.'

At this point, Hester with her dogs came round the corner towards the house, and Venetia in a fluster, clambered back into her car. 'I'm always happy to give you a lift,' she called to Amos as she drove away.

'You're keeping dangerous company these days,' Hester kidded him, then waved to Eve at the open window.

Amos tipped his head back to look up. As he saw Eve, a

familiar red swept over his face. He grunted at Hester and shambled indoors.

'What's all this domestic stuff?' Hester bawled up, miming window cleaning.

'It's the sun's fault. Shows all the marks.' As Eve called down, she saw Cheryl approaching with Troy in his buggy. Thank the good Lord for that, she thought.

Hester, too had been concerned. 'Where have you been, girl? We were all worried about you.'

'None of your business.' Cheryl stuck her jaw out. Then she changed tack. 'I just went down Yarmouth. That's all. With a friend.'

'But you didn't make arrangements for Troy.'

'My Mum always have him.' Cheryl's strapless top revealed a new rose tattoo on one shoulder. Her eyes sparkled.

'Come and have some coffee and tell me about it. And about Troy. I'm concerned about you both, you know,' Hester said, patting Cheryl's cheek. 'I'll just put my boys in the back.' She turned to wave to Eve. 'You, too.'

August

Mum. I managed to lug my 27kg rucksack to the airport at Saigon and loaded it on without having to pay excess. My shoulder muscles will be massive by the time I come home. Arrived in Hong Kong and caught a shuttle bus. The view was great. The skyline is full of huge skyscrapers, office blocks and stores with their neon lights blazing. People were still shopping and it was late evening. Now I'm in a place with a kettle and tea bags, which is great. But I'm feeling really grotty from the malaria pills and am sick and have lost my appetite. Have decided I'll stop taking them as I feel so vile. I think Hong Kong and Tokyo are fairly malaria free, but I shall probably have to start taking them again in India. I'll squirt myself with anti-mosquito spray instead. Am in an extremely noisy cybercafé, surrounded by Chinese boys playing loud computer games. The noise of machine guns and shouting is horrible. Will have to go before my ear drums burst. Lots of love from barfing sickliness Jez

Jez. I should imagine that cities are malaria free. Am sure you're making the right decision about the pills. On the subject of drugs, do be careful that your drinks aren't spiked with a "date-rape" drug. The newspapers here are full of references to them. Very worrying. I guess that Hong Kong is an elegant place. Here, anything goes, and that suits me. I've just bought a pair of scarlet shorts (very brief) and matching crop top for next to nothing in the town's best emporium, so that's my everyday holiday outfit. Life's pretty good in the sun here. Much love, M.

Shipden was noisy, full of families on holiday at the beginning of August. Smiling groups carrying red, blue and yellow buckets and spades marched through the little streets towards the beach. Swimmers splashed in the warm sea. Ice cream-eating children caught the same crabs, again and again, from the pier. A strong scent of fish and chips hung around certain corner cafes.

Eve didn't spend much time in the place. She and Choker, controlled by the depth of feeling in their liaison, met frequently in a quiet lane on the edge of town: in ferny copses, the depths of woods, isolated sandy beaches and remote salt marshes. They made love fast, breathlessly, and without taking themselves too seriously, laughing frequently.

From the back of his speeding bike, she admired blond harvested fields, high white hogweed and brilliant blue skies. Everything brighter, more vivid. She behaved impulsively, excited by the clandestine.

They were like-minded, valuing their independence, not wanting any commitment but enjoying being together. Eve never rang him, never mentioned his wife, never asked him questions, was always discreet and felt in control. But she thought about him: about his penetrating stare, muscular forearms, deep voice.

He telephoned frequently, behaved affectionately and one evening gave her a gift of Cartier gold and diamond earrings, which she at first refused, but eventually accepted. He implied that he and Venetia had not been sexually intimate for years. Eve always changed the subject when he mentioned his life or asked her about her past.

Yet once she spoke about herself. They were sitting in the corner of a city restaurant after a long meal. It was late and she had drunk a good deal of brandy. He was sober and staring at her intently.

'Why won't you talk about your past?' He stroked her bare arm.

The candles flickered. 'Mine's an ordinary life. Unexceptional. I made the mistake of marrying once, but it didn't last. He was a bully, a man who liked confrontations. I called him "The Dictator". He made me utterly miserable, so I ditched him.' She stared at the swirling liquid in her large glass.

'What about your childhood?'

'I was an only child. My mother didn't bother about me much. She used to give me away. Told me once she didn't need a crying baby, so she gave me to anyone who'd have me. Neighbours or strangers in the street who admired me. Anyone really. For half an hour, an evening, a fortnight, once for three months. But apparently, they always brought me back in the end. By the time I could speak, I could make a fuss and talk my way out of it. And anyway, by then she took to me and didn't want to get rid of me, she said. It was quite an admission for her. She had her virtues. An attractive young woman like that. I was a problem. I took a lot of risks. Didn't care. But that was after I left home.' She drank more brandy. 'I was innocent once. A child in a world of daydreams, fantasising about magic, thinking I must really be a princess. The usual sort of thing. Then came a bad experience. The dark age.'

'How do you mean?'

'I can't talk about it.'

He stared in her eyes. 'Have you ever? Talked about it?'

'No. I couldn't.'

He held her hands. 'You could write about it.'

'No.'

'Yes. It's much easier. You'll see. Just in simplified form, a few words. The bare essentials. Exorcize the experience that way. I do it all the time.'

'Really?'

'Mm. It helps. Look, I've got to go and make a couple of calls. I'll be a little while. Take this.' He tore a page from his notebook and brought out a biro. 'Write it down.' He stood, bent over and kissed her on the mouth. 'Back soon.'

She watched him cross the room, wondering if she could do as he suggested.

After a while she began an ugly scribbling on the piece of lined paper. She wrote quickly without thinking about the words, just letting them tumble and arranging themselves one after the other. Then she finished and folded the paper over and over into a tiny rectangle. She threw it in the ashtray.

He returned, and without saying anything, looked about for the bit of paper. When he saw it, he picked it up and unwrapped it. She put a warning hand over his. But he ignored it and read what she'd written in silence.

My dark age muscled in with the stubbled stranger who stalked me in winter woods through bars of light. He caught my puppy, twisted her neck and threw the yapped out remnant with a small splash in the river. Ordered me to stop crying tossed me down took all he wanted of the soft child I was then. Hurting, unable to scream I could only wait for the end of everything expecting to be lost in that cold earth for ever. He left with his stink of sweat smoke pubs his stained hard hands his dirty boots heavy on the fallen leaves when distant walkers passed. Then bruised and choked I ran home with bloody thighs and empty lead. Said my bitch had drowned. An accident. Nothing else. For shame until today I never told a soul.

Watching him read her words, she felt vulnerable and exposed. She wondered what he was thinking. His expression didn't change.

He sighed. 'This is a poem,' he said. Seconds passed. 'Do you want to keep it?'

'No.'

'Then it's gone for ever.' He held it to a candle flame where it burned steadily and became ash. 'Extinguished.'

'Part of the past,' she said. 'Done with. Forgotten.' Her eyes glittered. She thought to herself, those who have been violated often end up alone. Because it's safe. When one's afraid, it's difficult to trust men. Do I really trust this man? She put down her empty glass. 'Let's go now.'

A few days later she came home from a church concert, her head full of the stirring notes of Charpentier's Te Deum and Bach's Cantata 147. Having said goodnight on the corner of the street, she ran up the stairs and entered her flat, singing 'Herz und Mund und Tat und Leben' and went to put her new earrings away in her wooden jewellery box.

There wasn't much in there: some moonstone items, a gold chain, bangles and bits of spangly costume jewellery. She looked for her best piece, an antique sapphire and diamond ring. It wasn't there. Searching frantically, she turned first the contents of the box on her bed, then the dressing table drawers. She remembered putting it back in its place the night Hester had been given the dog painting.

What had happened since then? Leo had arrived. Instantly she knew that he must have taken it. Experience had taught her that he had no scruples. No one else had access to her bedroom and nothing else had been stolen. She felt raw with fury. The ring meant so much. It was her only possession that Leo could get good money for in London. Not that it was so valuable. Only to her.

Bastard, she thought, I helped him, how could he? She imagined tracking him down, confronting him. She rehearsed what she would say. But he would deny all knowledge. That ring was the only thing she'd owned from her mother. It had been destined for Jez. Eve vowed revenge.

For a week or two she had been so happy with Choker she hadn't thought so much about her daughter. She still woke every morning thinking about her, but her concern had lost its sharp edge. With the loss of her ring, all her old despondencies returned.

Loss of things. This was a small loss. But the sacrifice of people was so much worse. How could the misery be endured?

She thought of the latest missing girl and the child's parents. How she would feel if a policewoman came knocking on her door? Panic and despair. How she would look in the woman's pitying eyes and hear a voice telling her that her daughter was dead. A bleakness. Shock and grief. All the worst fears realised. She imagined the body in the woods, black rooks calling above, flapping from the trees.

Clearing up the mess she'd made, she turned to her computer.

Mum. Everyone here in Hong Kong is very slim/little and weedy looking as though they will fall over in a small wind. I feel like an elephant. Caught the ferry to Hong Kong Island and ambled. There is a huge set of escalators going up the hill into a suburb of expensive housing and restaurants, so I played on the escalators and did some window shopping. Here people take their appearance seriously so I felt scruffy. Caught the Peak Tram into the hills and it was incredibly steep. The view was great. Was invited to a Salsa Club by a nice Australian bloke and there were lots of European and American men with their tiny Thai/ Philippino/Malaysian/Chinese wives/girlfriends. They got completely blasted on Margarita cocktails and when the live salsa band came on, danced around letting their hair down. It was a riot. Have to say that trying to salsa in great big galumphing trekker sandals isn't easy! But good fun and everyone was terribly friendly. I was by far the most sober person in the group as everyone else was pie-eyed. See, I am taking care of myself. Love, Jez XXX

Jez. Glad to hear you are looking after yourself. Cheryl and Darren here are inclined to get drunk from time to time and we worry about Troy. Cheryl doesn't get aggressive, just falls asleep, but as she never locks her door, Hester and I go and sort her out. Darren acts strangely and I've been known to help him up the stairs into his flat. Normally they're fine. I'm in the pink, or rather tanned brown. I think of all the time I wasted in the polluted city, breathing in noxious fumes. It's wonderful living on the coast, all this fresh air makes me feel really alive. Take care, M.

Eve walked up the track by crooked pine trees, enjoying the sensation of Choker's hot hand and arm round her waist. She felt the sun's rays on her head. The two had swum in the glittering North Sea waves and made love among the deserted sand dunes.

'So, what did you say?' She yawned.

Choker stopped and kissed her. 'Nothing at all.'

She smiled.

'I forgot to tell you,' he said. 'I have to go to a literary festival tomorrow. In the West Country. Deadly boring. But I get paid for it. Workshops, readings, that sort of stuff. But I'll be back a week on Wednesday night. Shall I see you on the Thursday morning?' He put his arm lightly round her shoulders.

'Fine. Are you going by train tomorrow?' She yawned again.

'Am I boring you?'

'Absolutely.'

'Mm. Yes I am taking the train.'

'Perhaps we could go down to London together. I was planning to go to Tate Modern for some art history research anyway.' She pushed strands of hair out of her eyes.

'Great. Shall we catch the 8 o'clock?'

'I'll meet you at the station.'

Where the track met the lane, they stood by his motorbike and packed their towels.

Eve saw high in the vivid, cloudless sky, swallows swooping and circling.

A dark car came soundlessly, slowly round the corner. A well-known, round face stared out, the jaw dropping. But the car continued past them and out of sight.

'Christ!' Choker, aghast at seeing his wife in the wrong place, crammed his helmet down over his head, leapt on the bike and revved. 'What on earth is she doing here?'

Eve, stuck half crouching as though to conceal herself, could only move slowly, like a character in a nightmare.

'Get on! Get on, girl!' he shouted.

They roared off in the opposite direction to Venetia.

The next morning Eve waited for him at the little station. She looked at her watch. Almost eight. He was cutting it fine. She bit her lip as she heard noisy vibration up the line.

The small train rattled in and a couple of people stepped out as a young girl climbed aboard. The couple walked away. There was no sign of Choker.

'D'you want this one?' called the guard to Eve, solitary on the platform.

She shook her head. The doors closed and the train rumbled off.

Blasted man, she thought. Why can't he make the effort to be on time?

The minutes passed slowly as she paced waiting. He never turned up.

What's going on? She banged her heels on the concrete and fidgeted. Eventually she caught the next slow train to the nearest city to catch the connection to London. Thinking he might just be at that station, she searched for him. But he was nowhere.

The air-conditioned train sped to Liverpool Street station. On the way she drank coffee from polystyrene beakers and stared through the window unseeing, wondering what he could be up to, alternating between anger and anxiety towards him. She imagined different conversations he might have had with his wife.

Her forbidden relationship with Choker made her high—as if on a drug. Being with him was exciting. Yet she couldn't be quite as unemotional about him as she'd earlier hoped. She admitted to herself that she did care about him.

I'm going to have to make up my mind about this man, she thought. I'd like to know just how much he feels for me. And despite what he says, does he really have any intimate relationship with Venetia?

Her train pulled in to Liverpool Street Station.

In the few months since she'd left, the city appeared to have become dirtier and busier. She spent a couple of hours at Bankside talking to an art historian, then, satisfied, packed her work papers. She thought about trying to track Leo and confront him about her ring. But she had no idea where he could be living and lacked the energy to attempt to find the name of his agent.

She decided to go to the West End to look at the shops. The streets buzzed with tourists: smartly dressed Japanese groups and European and Antipodean youngsters staggering under great backpacks. It was hot and humid, the sullen air filled with vehicle exhaust. Parks filled with people, some sitting on the grass eating sandwiches, others lying sleeping in the shade of trees. Teenage office girls, prone, with arms raised, worshipped the sun. Men sat on pavements outside pubs, and weary, white-faced shop-workers behind counters showed their longing for escape.

Eve felt lonely in the crush of humanity. I should be with Choker, she kept thinking, not wandering on my own. I need his arm in mine, his funny conversation. Such thoughts surprised her, until some weeks ago she'd been content to be alone, preferred it. I mustn't get dependent on him for my happiness. That way misery lies, she decided. But without him, the city and its inhabitants for the first time seemed alien and ugly.

On burning Oxford Street, she felt giddy and wandered through cool department stores flooded with scents. Everything was far too expensive and not worth buying anyway.

She went on the Tube and once again saw distorted,

reflected faces staring from the glass. She had spent too many years doing just that—sitting in a dirty, odorous, rattling Underground train surrounded by strangers—she realised it was not what she wanted.

A man sitting further up the carriage had unruly black hair and a straight nose in profile like Choker's. But when he stood, she saw his full-face was different. She averted her gaze.

In a hurry she returned to what she knew she could call home. She could hardly wait to get back to the fresh air and brightness of Shipden, where strangers smiled and spoke, and she had her space around her only Choker could come near.

An overcast morning. She woke late and, slower, trudged downstairs to shop. As she reached the hall Hester emerged from her flat, and they walked down the street under a slate sky.

'You don't look yourself today,' Eve observed.

'Who do I look like, then?'

Eve, who thought Hester seemed particularly haggard and old, with dark shadows under her red-rimmed eyes, didn't like to say.

'I'm very concerned.' Hester had left her basket and the dogs behind. 'I'm going to the police station. I had a phone call from a woman I know. She said that very early this morning a body was found washed up on the east end of the beach.'

'A child?'

'No. A youngish man with dark hair. Wearing black leathers.'

Time stopped. Eve could hardly breathe. She couldn't trust herself to speak. She knew exactly who Hester thought it might be.

Is this Venetia's work? Eve's first reaction was guilt-impelled.

'Of course,' said Hester, 'it could be a suicide. Or a drowned sailor. These things happen here.' She didn't look at Eve. 'I must get on.' She hurried off.

From the cliffs Eve, in panic, stared down at the beach. There was no sign of a body or a police presence. All looked normal. By now the sand was filled with noisy families ignoring the clouds. People walked on the pier. Nothing out of place. Only her heart hammered unevenly, out of sorts with surrounding events.

She tried to remember what Choker had told her about his plans. A Literary Festival? But where? And surely such things weren't held in August when people were likely to be on holiday. Since she'd known him, she'd been happy to accept whatever he told her. Now she wondered if he'd lied. All she could feel was fear. He hadn't been in touch. Could he be dead?

Sea bindweed crept low to the ground under bushes of buckthorn. She stared at the foliage until everything blurred and she could only walk wearily back.

In the afternoon she went out to buy the late edition of the local paper. There was only a tiny mention of an unidentified body washed up on the beach in the early hours of the morning. It's the height of the tourist season, she thought, this would hardly be on the front page.

What could she do? Ring Venetia? Impossible. She didn't want to talk to Hester either.

She felt sick. The hours ticked by uselessly.

September

Mum. Hong Kong is good. I went to a seafood place with rows of live fish and shellfish in tanks. You pick what you want and someone plucks it out and shoves it in a plastic bowl for your inspection. If you like the look of it they cook it for you. It was all a bit too barbaric for me. The poor old lobsters and octopi were trying desperately to get out of their tanks. Ghastly. My new Australian friend chose scallops and prawns for me, to be cooked in garlic, but I would have felt too guilty eating them. I just had vegetables in the end. The people next to us were demolishing all sorts of stuff, plates with feet sticking out and anemones with massive spikes. The Chinese find dog very tasty and breed them for cooking in the same way we breed cattle and sheep. It's really great being back in a big city again and I'm enjoying being a tourist and seeing a bit of culture. However, I'm trying not to spend much money. Off to Tokyo tomorrow and have been reading my little 'Rough Guide'. I think it will be terribly expensive so I'm not going to stay a long time and have paid for accommodation at a youth hostel in advance. Must go as I'm back in this repulsive internet café full of children playing war games on the computers. The noise is really astonishingly ear-bursting and I can't hear myself think. Big kisses, Jez

Jez. What's your Australian friend like? Is he huge with a big appetite, like that man from Adelaide we met in Fulham? Will you see him again, do you think? I remember you said that you thought Australia was full of male chauvinists, but one can't generalise. Any man, of any nationality, who can imagine what it's like to be someone else, is worth cultivating. A bit of sensitivity goes a long way. Love, M.

The early September sky glowed deep blue and the little streets and long beaches of Shipden were still packed with families eager to make the most of their seaside holidays. They continued to roll in on the Bittern line, on coaches and cars from the city, the Midlands, the north and south. The scent of candyfloss and hot oil hung around the streets and the sand and pebbles divided by dark groynes were still filled with toddlers digging and old people paddling, exposing their misshapen tuber legs.

There was still no news of Choker. Eve had been to the police station and rung journalists working on the local paper, but no one was giving out information, even if they knew anything. She didn't like to distress Hester by talking about the mystery.

She tried to work at preparing art history courses, but her mind wouldn't settle. Frantic with worry, at last she threw her pen down, swept her papers together in a pile on the table, and left the flat.

Cheryl leaned against the high garden wall by the road. 'Hi, Eve,' she called through a cloud of smoke. She stubbed her cigarette on the stone gatepost. 'D'ya know more about that bloke drowned at sea? The one who came up on the shore?'

'No. Who was he, do you know?'

'No idea. Wish I'd found him. Never seen a stiff yet.'

Eve thought, somewhere in the world someone has lost a lover and parents their son. Do they know already or are they still enjoying their lives? She walked slowly away.

She went down a back street and through a yard to the workshop where her paintings were being framed for the hotel. But they were nowhere near finished, so she decided to walk along the top of the cliffs to the next village.

Heading east with the sun on her face and the breeze ruffling her unwashed, uncombed hair, she stepped close to the cliff edge. Far below children ran in and out of the sea, their calls mixing with gulls' cries. On her right, intent golfers paraded the hilly fairways. She passed friendly dog walkers and lone hikers who greeted her. There was no escape from people.

'Where are you, Choker?' she called angrily to the sea, which restlessly threw its waves at the stones. Her throat ached. She stumbled away from the cliff top.

As she approached the village a car drew up next to the elegant, white-painted Edwardian hotel and someone she recognised climbed out. It was Simon Kirk, one of her students, a young man who'd given up studying law to train for a new career. He was clever and interested in art history, finding pleasure in research.

'Hello,' she called. 'Congratulations on your result.' She noticed his immaculate pale linen suit and, conscious of her torn denim skirt, smoothed it, feeling like a peasant. A role reversal.

'Good to see you, Eve. Thanks. All due to you. You're a great teacher. Infected us all with your enthusiasm. I followed your instructions to the letter. I hear the whole group did well.' His smile displayed gleaming teeth. 'Do you live around here?'

'Not far. I just walked over from Shipden. It's quieter here.'

'Come and have a congratulatory drink with me in this place.' He waved a hand at the hotel. 'We can go in the garden.'

Sitting in a soft chair, with a cold glass of Buck's Fizz in hand, a view of the sea, pink and white roses trembling all around, and a good-looking youth staring at her with interest, she relaxed a little. 'So, what are you doing now?' She gazed up at him through her eyelashes and tangled locks.

'I'm off to Florence shortly. Getting to grips with the Renaissance. I'm really looking forward to it.' He looked at her legs. 'What tiny ankles you have.' He raised his eyes. 'And wrists.'

'What brings you here?' She smiled, realizing that he was

the same age as Jez.

'Meeting my aunt. She's collected a list of contact addresses in Italy for me and some parcels to take out there.' He glanced behind her and stood. 'Here she comes now.'

Eve turned, and to her horror, saw Venetia approach. It was too late to do anything but sit there and fix a polite smile to her face.

Venetia frowned. 'Hello, Simon darling.'

He kissed her on both cheeks. 'This is Eve Key, my art teacher at college. Venetia Chakour.' He flexed his long fingers towards her. 'We met by chance.'

Eve put out her hand. Venetia's felt soft and cool, studded with sharp rings.

'How do you do.' Simon's aunt, expensively dressed in yellow silk, didn't look at her.

Eve knew she'd been recognised. Aware of her tatty beach clothes, flip flops revealing grubby toes, and her lack of makeup, she felt at a disadvantage once more. Would Venetia say anything to her nephew about the last time the two women had seen each other?

But Eve was dismissed as though she didn't exist. Venetia simply turned her chair round and sat facing the young man. 'Now, Simon. When are you off?'

'Next week. I understand you and Marc are going away shortly, too. The Caribbean. Is that right?'

This was news to jealous Eve, staring at Venetia's shoulder.

'Ah, yes. Provided, of course, he turns up in time to catch the flight.' Venetia pulled her sunglasses from the top of her head. 'He arranged this surprise holiday for us. We've both been working too hard so we need to have some special time to ourselves.'

Eve squirmed. Did Venetia know where Choker was? Had they had a fight? She imagined the husband and wife attacking each other over revelations about Choker's affair.

Eve willed Simon to ask about his uncle. He didn't.

'I've so much to do before we go.' Venetia rummaged in a leather bag. 'I brought these things for you to take to Italy.' She leaned close to him. 'I think we ought to order now. Service can be slow here.' She picked up a menu lying on the table. 'The bouillabaisse is usually reasonable.'

'How about you, Eve?' Simon turned to include her. 'Would you like to have lunch with us?'

'That's very kind. But I'm afraid I can't today.' She drained her glass and stood. 'Thanks, and have a great time in Florence.' Grinning at him, she ignored his aunt.

As she walked away, she felt them both staring at the back of her short skirt. She had to concentrate hard to walk in a straight line.

As soon as she left the hotel, she found herself thinking, I must tell Choker about that. Then remembered with a shock she couldn't.

Hungering for bouillabaisse, she made her way to the village shop, then ate a huge bar of chocolate on the slow walk home.

Slowly she entered Strand House as Cheryl came through the hall. She held the door open for the girl to push the buggy out, and for the first time noticed Cheryl's prominently curved stomach. Pregnant again, she thought, and had an unexpected surge of relief that it wasn't her. She had the stomach cramps to prove it.

As she came upstairs Amos blocked her way on the landing outside his door. For the first time he looked straight at her.

'It's my birthday.' He flushed as usual.

'Congratulations.' She attempted to pass.

But he put out a damp hand and touched her hip.

She couldn't help flinching. She couldn't bear his closeness.

'Come and have a drink with me. Please? Half past eight

at mine.' He could see her reluctance as she backed away. 'The Tomblings are coming. You int bin to mine yet.'

That's certainly true, she thought, and wondered what his flat was like. She felt a surge of pity. He couldn't help his appearance. As a good neighbour she ought to be polite and could just have a quick drink and a chat to Grace and Vernon. Perhaps she could learn to understand and like him better. Such a pathetic character. 'Yes, thank you. I'll be there.' She sprang past him, running up the last flight.

At ten to nine, changed into a long skirt, demure blouse, and with her hair piled into a knot on top of her head, she knocked on his door.

'Happy birthday!' She offered him a wrapped bottle of wine, not wishing to give him anything more personal.

He put it in his galley kitchen without a word and led her into his living room.

She saw it as an empty cardboard box, with beige picture-free walls, brown carpet, a three-piece suite in fawn mock leather plastic and an old-fashioned, bulbous TV surrounded by stacks of videos on the floor. The room was grubby and permeated with the stale smell of mouldy food. Light streamed from one unshaded bulb dangling from the ceiling. The only colour came from the closed grey curtains patterned with orange daisies.

He noticed the object of her gaze. 'My Mum give me them. Years ago.'

'Does she live near?'

'Dead now. And Dad. Both gone.'

'I'm sorry.' In the silence she tried to change the subject. 'How's work?'

'Work's work. It int pleasure.' He sniffed. 'I bin to the police today. Somebody's bin stealing my letters.'

'What makes you think that?' All the mail that came to the house was left on the hall windowsill in separate piles for each flat occupant.

'Nearly nathin come for me now.'

'But who would take your letters?'

'That Darren. He's a waster.' He held up a sticky bottle of sweet sherry, which had been standing on the floor by the videos. 'Have some o this,' he invited.

She hesitated, reluctant.

'Tha's all I got.'

'Thank you. Just a little, please.'

He stomped slowly to his kitchen with the bottle.

He returned with two birthday cards, which he placed importantly on the television set, then he left again.

One card had a picture of teddy bears, the other a gaudy racing car. If she'd bought him a card, what would she have chosen? But she couldn't think of anything that might suit his personality.

There were no books or magazines, no ornaments of any sort, no cushions or comfort. The curtains moved slightly in the breeze from the open window.

From the kitchen came the blare of *I Heard it Through the Grapevine*.

Amos came back with a little radio playing and set it on the floor. 'I like 70s pop,' he said, turning Marvin Gaye up. '*My Love is Waiting* is my favourite,' Amos shouted. He retreated, before reappearing with two large, smeary tumblers of sherry.

I'll never get through all that, she thought, wishing the Tomblings would hurry up. 'Your good health.' She held up her glass and took a swig. It was as horrible as she'd feared, reminding her of childhood medicine.

'This is nice.' He lowered himself next to her on the slippery sofa, which creaked and sagged. He smiled, so close, revealing grotesquely buckled teeth. His breath was repellent.

For some time, she tried to get him to talk. But questioning him only resulted in responses of 'yes' or 'no'. She edged into the corner of the sofa, willing Vernon or Grace to knock on the door.

'Tomorrow I'm goo'n to Lowestoft for my holiday. Bed and breakfast. I goo every year,' he offered at last.

'Great. I hope you have good weather.'

The pop music boomed. He couldn't hear what she said, so moved ever nearer to her. She was conscious of his bulk filling her space, his bulging eyes level with her breasts. She tried to hold her breath, then launched into inconsequential monologues about Shipden and their neighbours.

He stared at her silently, nodding his big head and waving fat little hands in time to the tunes.

She made a move to leave. But he said quickly, 'Wait. The Tomblings will soon be here.'

'Just five minutes, then I'll have to go.' She subsided again and drank more and more from the dirty glass.

As both their glasses were together at their feet, occasionally he picked hers up to drink from it.

'That's mine!' she said angrily, snatching it, not being able to bear the thought of him sharing her glass. Was he making a genuine mistake?

Her head hurt and she had difficulty in focussing. She forced herself to look at him. No amount of alcohol would make him more appealing. But why was she getting so woozy so quickly?

She attempted to get up. 'I must...' but couldn't finish. She leaned back, aware he was going out with the empty glasses and returning with full ones. Determined not to drink more, she shut her eyes. It's no good being sorry for the poor bugger, she thought. I was stupid enough to get in this situation, now I must get the hell out of it. But she felt so ill and giddy and her aching head was so muddled she could hardly move. She slumped.

When she regained consciousness, the radio was still playing and her head still hurt. She opened her eyes to the too-bright light shining down on Amos snoring on the floor, his bald head against her feet.

Recoiling, she noticed that her blouse was half unbuttoned. She managed to stand at the second attempt. Clutching the sofa arm, she peered at her watch. Two thirty-one am. She grabbed her bag and stumbled out.

Back in the safety of her own bathroom she checked her underwear. All was as it should be. Feeling nauseous at the thought of Amos near her, she collapsed into bed.

In the morning she heard him banging about below and then leave the house. She forced herself to get out of bed and watch him from the window as he shuffled away. He looked white and sick. She felt contempt. What had he been playing at, last night? Had he put something in her drink? Rohypnol? Those 'roofies'? She'd warned Jez about a so-called 'date rape' drug called—what was it? Gamma hydroxybutyrate or GHB? Something like that. Liquid ecstasy. She'd read about it. And there was a prescription pain killer, Oxycodone, she'd heard that men used to take advantage of girls. Whatever it was, Amos had been affected too. What a gross moron he was. She cursed herself for being so gullible. That was the last time she'd feel pity for a man like that. As soon as he came back to his flat, she'd go down and have it out with him. He couldn't be allowed to continue in that way.

Later in the day she met Grace at the baker's.

'It was Amos Postle's birthday yesterday. I went to his flat in the evening. Did he invite you and Vernon?'

'No, dear. He's never asked us. We've never been in there. He's such a shy man. Very self-conscious of his appearance. Poor man can't help what he looks like. But I don't think he encourages friendship.' Grace tucked her bag of rolls into her shopping trolley and walked on.

October

Eve woke early to go for a run. On the beach, shingle rattled in the waves as she watched tankers slowly moving on the edge of the sky. High above, silent aircraft ploughed white trails in the blue. She'd still heard nothing from Choker, though she dreamed about him frequently.

Everything had cooled. The morning was misty and she could hardly see the watery sun she ran towards. Dew trembled on spiders' webs that clung to promenade railings. The constant swishing of the sea made a rhythm to her steps and in the pale haze distant waves were like dark logs rolling in. The sharp tang of seaweed a familiar accompaniment to the thudding in her throat and the pounding of her feet.

Later, on the train to the city, she watched the changing landscape. Pigs emerged from the fog, heads down, snuffling in the whiteness like dream creatures. As the sun broke through the vapour, dark trees made patterns against a pale grey sky and rooks flapped over trailing telegraph wires. Gulls pecked the rich, brown earth of dug fields.

Rain and gale-filled days followed. She continually thought about Jez, imagining her a solitary figure striding through foreign cities.

Mum. It's colder here in Tokyo and there's not so much internet access. Sorry I haven't been in touch so much. I searched high and low for the one I'm using now. Tokyo is massive and they have an enormous train network that is incredibly complicated. Managed to find my way to the hostel at Asakusa after changing trains a few times and asking strangers for directions. It's amazing the sort of actions you end up doing when trying to ask a question when no one understands what you're saying. It's more like a hotel and tends to be used by businessmen, though it's advertised in the youth hostelling handbook as a hostel and is cheaper than most of the hotels here, so that's good. Asakusa is quite vibrant with the shops open and stallholders selling their wares by the light of lanterns. In central Tokyo all the staff in the big department stores bow to you and greet you as you walk past. It took me by surprise. When they started to bow, I leapt sideways as I thought someone really important was entering the building behind me. They must have thought I was mad leaping around all over the place. I'm still trying to find the Imperial Palace; I know it's here somewhere. Must go. Love Jez.

Jez. I miss you. I was surprised you couldn't find much internet access in Japan of all places. But I expect most people there have their own computers. I'm having a quiet time right now. Last night I sorted the unframed old photos of you and stuck them in an album (very tasteful tapestry cover) in chronological order, from fat babyhood upwards. You'll approve. Any snap slightly less than brilliant, eg the one with chocolate-smeared face and the one where you're looking demented under that Easter egg knitted hat, has been left out. This is one bulging album. Hope you find your palace soon. Love always, M.

More days passed without a word from Choker. Eve continued to make phone calls to the police about the body on the beach, but discovered nothing. She tried, unsuccessfully, not to think about him. She missed his physical company.

One day a card depicting the Duomo, Santa Maria del Fiore, came to her at college. It was from Simon who was finding Florence wonderful. She envied him. It made her think that her new students were dull compared to those she'd taught the term before.

Shipden's streets had emptied as the summer finished, and the locals, including Eve, once more enjoyed the tranquillity.

The flat below had been agreeably silent for some time.

Amos had been on his two-week annual holiday. She was frustrated at being unable to show him how furious she was at his behaviour and she rehearsed the questions she would ask on his return.

She spent more time with Hester, who told her one day that the body found on the shoreline had still not been identified, but was probably a foreign seaman. 'A friend in the press let me know. Thinks he came off a tanker a few miles out. Covered in tattoos of anchors and mermaids. Expect he got pissed and fell overboard. Poor bastard. There'll be an inquest. His body had been in the water for a few weeks.'

But although Hester was relieved, she now showed her annoyance with Choker. 'These chapters need editing. I need his help. What's he playing at? Where is he? He's not been in touch. So unreliable, that man. I've a good mind to pack in this writing business.' She snorted. 'It's not my metier, after all. I just remember what happened and he sorts it all out.'

Then something else took their minds off thoughts of Choker.

Darren hadn't been around for some time and the top storey of Strand House had been quiet without him. Eve picked up a local paper left on her train and read it on the way home. '*A heroin addict seen dealing drugs by undercover police officers in Shipden was jailed for two years yesterday. Darren Gooch, 23, of Strand House, Coast Road, Shipden admitted supplying heroin and possessing it with intent to supply. He was seen passing a package and arrested. He was searched and had 13 grams of heroin hidden in his sock. He admitted that he had been dealing for three days and had sold wraps to pay for his addiction.*'

The moment she got in the house, she told Hester.

'Ah, well,' said Hester. 'Once you start that stuff, it's the devil to stop. I thought he seemed ill last time I saw him. I don't think he's got family round here. I'll see if I can visit.'

When Eve reached the top landing, she could tell that the police had been to his flat; his door was shut for the first time since she'd moved in. Later, a man in uniform called to question her on Darren's drug habit and she was truthfully able to deny knowledge. Despite searching his place and taking the speakers apart, no heroin had been found.

Days later, a middle-aged man in a navy boiler suit came in an old van and cleared out Darren's few possessions.

The weather turned cold and Eve tried to turn her heating on without success. The plumber she called told her it would cost a good deal to repair.

That puts paid to all the money I earned from the hotel paintings, she thought, swearing. She'd been hoping to get away for Christmas. Imagining living in a cold flat, waking with a chilly face, shivering and shuddering all winter, she told the plumber to go ahead.

She began painting again, this time for her own pleasure, a series of large oil abstracts based on the shapes of shells in greys, white and blue. Moving from figurative styles to abstraction, and back, came easily to her. She became absorbed in her work.

One evening her phone rang as she was about to have an early night, tired from a long day's teaching, attending 'special' (in her terms 'boring') meetings with dull colleagues, and writing student references.

'Is that you, Eve?' Choker's husky voice echoed inside her head.

At first, she was flooded with relief. Then came recriminations. She'd been half demented with worry. 'Where have you been? There's been no word from you for ages.' Shit, she thought, I sound just like a nagging wife.

'Did you miss me, beauty?'

'As much as you missed me.'

'I'm really sorry I haven't been in touch for so long.' The pause lengthened. 'I've been in St Lucia. Writing mostly. In a villa on Windward Ridge. Looking out at the ocean and catching the breeze. Wish you could have been with me. But

I've produced some amazing work.'

She was taken aback by his casualness. 'That's good. I've been busy too, back at the college. My nose to the grindstone,' she said, coolly. Then, as anger flared again, 'Why didn't you let me know what was happening? There's been not one phone call from you.'

'I'm sorry. My life's been chaotic. I haven't been myself.' He paused. 'I must see you, Eve. I'm at the Dragon. Come now, please.'

'I was on my way to bed.'

'You get my drift.'

She felt the usual frisson and couldn't help herself from speedily readying to meet him.

Choker sat in an out of the way corner, almost hidden by trailing plants. Initially she didn't recognise him, a stranger with a dark tan, a new black beard and a foreign ecru cashmere sweater. He stood.

'You look different,' she said after they embraced. 'Are you well?'

'I'm fine now.' He laughed. 'I've just been too lazy to shave.' His gaze raked her up and down. 'I'd forgotten just how eye-catching you are. My own Helen of Troy.'

She stared at two glasses on the table. 'What am I drinking?'

'Whisky and a surprise ingredient. You'll like it. Believe me. Sit here.' He pulled her next to him.

'You're a control freak ordering me about.'

'Too true, lover. But that's what you like. Admit it.' He smiled. 'But I did miss you. I'm sorry I couldn't meet you at the station as we arranged. I rang, but you'd already left. Seems an age ago.' He hugged her again. 'Now speak. What's been going on without me?'

'Hester thought you were drowned. She was very upset until she found out it was a foreign seaman who happened to fit your description. There wasn't much in the paper. An accident apparently.'

'I'll come and see her tomorrow without fail.'

Eve decided not to mention her experience with Amos or her meeting with Simon and Venetia. If Choker wanted to talk about his wife, he would do so in his own time. 'And Cheryl. I think she's pregnant again.'

He took a long, slow drink. 'She ought to have a termination.'

'How can you say such a thing?'

'There's not much maternal instinct there. Her boy doesn't have much of a life.'

'Who's his father?'

'Your guess is as good as mine. She turned up at Strand House around two years ago with the newborn baby. Her ma takes care of him a good deal, I believe.'

Eve looked round her and relaxed back into her seat. She knew she wouldn't get back to her flat until the early hours and prepared to enjoy herself. 'This whisky's very warming. There's more gossip. You won't have heard about Darren.'

November

Mum. I'm really enjoying Tokyo. The streets are clean and the people friendly. Everyone wears neat and tidy clothes for work and all the men wear suits and have tidy leather briefcases. It's like the West End of London without the filth and squalor and homeless people sitting round asking for money. The homeless ones here are neat and tidy with all their possessions organised in bags on trolleys, very sensible. Mind you, some young Japanese have brightly coloured hair and wear enormous platform shoes, but they're not scary like British youths with their tattoos and body piercings. I've been watching TV but can't understand it. The adverts make me laugh as the Japanese seem to be obsessed with their bowels and keep advertising things to keep you regular. The children's programmes are very funny. I watched one yesterday that had lots of little Japanese infants dressed up as big furry bees and ladybirds and they were all jumping up and down to music, very sweet. But everything in my room is so small. The bed is too short and when I have a shower, I keep hitting my head on the ceiling. The bathroom is so tiny I have to come out to get dried. Lots of love Jez XXX

Jez. I'm laughing thinking of you in your dolls' house. It's great to be tall and elegant. Wish I wasn't so short. I've just bought myself some new boots with very high heels, supremely cool and fashionable. However, quite useless for going to work in the winter. I'll be hobbling about in the slush, wishing I'd bought flat, sheepskin, old-lady jobs. You know me. Look after yourself. Love, M.

November wind battered the rooftops and scudded up the waves. From under a nearby horse-chestnut tree, Eve had collected glossy conkers to keep moths from her clothes cupboard. Now the last yellow leaves fell from the branches to lie among red and bronze heaps of scratchy, dead foliage on pavements and gutters.

The first mild morning she opened her window and leaned out, enjoying the soft air on her face. In sheltered gardens she could see wind-blown roses flowering and the vivid pink of nerine lilies.

Directly below Grace was hobbling about on the flat roof terrace above the first floor. This was a communal area. She had a couple of dozen containers and was busy replanting some with blue pansies. She pulled dead leaves from scarlet pelargoniums in pots.

'Sometimes these geraniums survive the winter out here,' she said to Eve. 'We don't get much frost by the sea.' All her plants were flourishing. She pulled out a few weeds and brushed the area. The eastern light behind her shone through her fine, silver hair, making it a halo. 'I'm finding it difficult to get up here, now, though. The blessed stairs are too steep for me. I don't know how long I can manage.'

As she spoke the door from the landing opened and, in a stained peach polyester dressing gown, Cheryl shuffled onto the terrace. She plonked herself on a plastic chair and swigged from a lager can.

'Where's Troy?' called Eve from her window.

'Asleep.' Cheryl yawned, red-faced.

Eve was sorry. The little boy always ran to her for a hug. He was talking, called his mother 'Churl' and his frequent cries of 'Bikit, Churl, Bikit!' echoed the stairwell.

'Should you be drinking that, dear?' Grace enquired, mildly.

'Why not?' Cheryl burped and pulling a tin box from her pocket, rolled a cigarette. She lit up and puffed smoke in Grace's direction.

'Because of your condition. It's not good.'

'What bloody condition?'

'Your interesting condition. Your pregnancy, dear.'

'S'not bloody interesting. S'a bloody nuisance.' Cheryl drained the can and threw it over the edge of the roof into the next-door garden.

Grace and Eve exchanged glances.

'Mind your own fucking business.' Cheryl staggered back inside and slammed the door behind her.

'Poor girl,' said Grace. 'I'll ask Hester to have a word. I think she needs some help and Hester's more tactful than I am.' She sat. 'I need a rest. Did you know someone's moving into Darren's flat?'

'I did hear something. But I'd better get going myself now. Bye Grace.' Eve closed her window.

On her way out she met a muscular man in his thirties carrying a tea chest up the stairs.

She waited on the landing for him to pass.

'Hi,' he said. 'I'm Knox.'

'As in the school of hard…' She noted his craggy face and self-assurance.

'No. As in Fort. Who are you?'

'Eve. Are you moving to number six?'

'That's right.' He continued up the stairs.

'I'm in number seven. See you later,' she called and ran down, feeling that things were improving.

She worried about trips she was organising for her students to visit art galleries. One morning unable to sleep, she got out of bed around 3am and stood at her uncurtained kitchen window looking down on the dark, wet roads and buildings. Everything was still and silent. Puddles trembled and gleamed silver and black. Gutters dripped.

Hearing the Strand House main door closing, she wondered who was also awake. A figure emerged and walked quickly away under the streetlights without a backward glance. Choker. Could it be? The man turned right and down a side street. At her window, Eve had a clear view of his progress.

Then the unmistakeable and unpreventable distant roar of his motorbike confirmed her suspicion. She opened her window and leaned out. Directly below, two floors down, Hester's bedroom window light shone faintly.

Could there be more to Hester's relationship with Choker than she had imagined? Had she been naïve to believe the two were merely friends? She breathed carefully; a pain knotted in her stomach. Hester was in her sixties, for heaven's sake. But why would Choker park his bike away from the house unless he didn't want anyone to know he was visiting? He frequently came to see Hester during the day, but wasn't shy of announcing his presence then: his bike always sat on the tarmac next to the wall round the side.

Do I have exclusive rights to this man? asked Eve of herself. And the answer always came back—certainly not. But sharing him with Hester as well as Venetia was out of the question. She pondered a while then swallowed pills and went back to bed where she fell into a deep and dream-free sleep.

The next evening as she returned from work, Hester was walking back from the beach with the dogs and they met outside the front door.

Hester's pink cheeks shone in the twilight. 'We've been for miles,' she called. 'Tide's out. I'm absolutely knackered.'

'How's the biography going?'

'I stopped a while back. Having a rest. Choker's got it to sort out in his own time.'

So they weren't working on that early this morning, Eve thought. 'Have you seen him recently?'

'Oh, the other day,' she said vaguely. 'Get down, boys.' The dogs fussed round the door. 'They want their supper.' She beamed and disappeared into her flat.

Eve plodded upstairs and dumped her heavy bags in the

kitchen. Loud banging noises like the rearrangement of furniture came from the adjacent flat. Then the whining sound of a drill. Her nerves on edge, she decided to go out to eat.

She sat on a cliff bench above the empty pier, eating fish and chips from paper under a street light. Tiny lights from distant barges on the horizon moved slowly through the dark. The breeze blew against her from the sea. If only Jez were with me, she wished. I'm so tired and lonely. I need to talk to Jez.

She trudged back. As she stood on the top landing in the warmth fumbling with her key, the door of flat six opened and Knox stepped out. 'I heard you coming home.' His cropped sandy hair was powdered white, he had paint on his chiselled cheekbones and prominent chin, and his bare feet and ankles were filthy. In a sweaty singlet and jogging bottoms, he appeared powerfully built and sinewy. 'Could you do me a neighbourly favour? Help me with some jobs? Just a few minutes, please? There are things one person can't do alone.' His wide smile and even teeth attracted her again. She noted his earlobes were almost nonexistent.

'Of course.' She entered the muddle of his flat and held a tape measure while he marked places on walls. She held bits of wood while he screwed shelves into place, and assisted with his electrical do-it-yourself. She admired the blinds on his windows.

'I don't understand curtains,' he said. 'All that feminine tat.'

Towering stacks of books dusted in plaster covered the floor. Metal filing cabinets and weight lifting equipment blocked the doorways. There was hardly room to move.

'What do you do?' she asked, threading flex round the skirting board for him.

'I'm just out of the army. And getting divorced. We'd only been married three weeks when she found someone she liked better. We were all in the same unit, which didn't help.' He paused. 'I met her through online dating. Never again.' He lifted an armchair lightly and balanced it on the table. 'I started at the university last month. A postgraduate course in business and management. I want a new career. Fresh start.'

'I don't do social media at all.' She stared around. 'Why did you come to Shipden?'

'I had a holiday here as a child. Really liked it. My father took me sea-fishing and I caught a sea bass with lugworm. I'll never forget it.' He picked up his box of tools. 'I want to get this place sorted out asap so I can get on with my course work. It's piling up.'

'It's over twenty miles to the university from here.'

'I know. I don't have to go in every day. Just once or twice a week, I reckon. I can work in the library there.'

'Is that your bicycle in the hall downstairs?'

'It is. Decent weather I cycle there.'

Hester and the Tomblings had shown a certain amount of disapproval of the bike parked on the carpet, but Eve didn't like to mention that.

'If it's peeing down, I use my old VW camper,' he continued. 'I've left it out of the way, by the washing line at the back.'

'There's not much going on here.' She passed him the pliers. 'It's very quiet. Not like the summer.'

'Suits me.'

She caught him staring at her unringed fingers. He glanced up. 'That's all finished. Thanks very much for your help. Some things can't be done single handed.'

'A pleasure.' She stood. 'I've a chocolate cake I bought today. Like to come next door for a piece?'

'You bet. My favourite.' He searched around. 'Somewhere here I've a cache of vodka. I'll bring a bottle. Goes a treat with cake.' He scratched his hairy forearm. 'I'm sorry I didn't introduce myself properly when I moved in. The fact is my father was called home the day after, so I had to rush up to Scotland.'

'Called home?'

His face dropped. 'He passed away. It was a real shock. And I had a lot of sorting out to do, both up there and here.'

'I'm sorry.'

'Thanks. I'm on my own now. Takes some getting used to. Not that I saw him much. It makes me realise that he must have been lonely. Poor old sod.'

The next afternoon, as she attempted to put her key in Strand House front door, it opened inwards. Two people blocked her way. The young man in a dark suit had a sheaf of papers tucked under his arm, and the bulky middle-aged woman held a heavy handbag of overlapping horny scales in front of her like armour. 'And where are the meters?' she asked the man, ignoring Eve as they passed.

The front door banged behind them. They moved off round the side of the house.

Eve, shocked, went slowly up the stairs. She thought she recognised the woman from a long time ago.

When she was a child, she had been taken frequently to visit her mother in Holloway prison. Inside, her incarcerated parent, a slight figure riddled with bitterness at 'the unfairness of life', would point out this particular woman warder as 'my enemy the pangolin'. She indicated to her daughter the 'outstanding schnozzle' of this uniformed woman officer who directed the inmates with bellows and sneers. The warder certainly had an amazingly long, pointed nose, in addition to silver close-cropped hair and beady, cold eyes.

This woman in Strand House had the same peculiar ant-eater snout.

Eve shivered. The pangolin would never recognise her. But she did not want to be reminded of her mother's miserable past. What was this unpleasant woman doing in Shipden? The man with wide lapels escorting her appeared to be an estate agent. Perhaps she was looking for a retirement flat for herself by the sea.

There was one flat vacant in the house, number three on the ground floor. As far as Eve knew, it was empty since March. Hester said it was owned by a man who lived in the Midlands and used it as a holiday flat. Eve had never seen him; he'd obviously not been able to make much use of it during the summer.

Eve worried about the pangolin. Then she realised, with a shock of relief, that this woman could not possibly be the one she'd seen in Holloway thirty years ago. It was just an uncanny resemblance. Years had passed. The pangolin would be old by now and look different.

Despite strangers coming and going through the hall occasionally, no one appeared to be moving into the ground floor flat.

There were days of mist, followed by rain and high winds. One grey morning on the train she contemplated the strange coastline, that desolation of earth and sky that was like no other. All seemed so wintry and depressing, foliage and wildlife dying. Then the sun broke free, colours deepened, and small fields widened to include men walking with shotguns over their arms. Dogs ran, noses to the grass, and sunlight gleamed along the gun barrels. Like a scene from an action film, it flashed before her, and was gone.

December

I'm not really a two-timer, Eve thought and laughed to herself at the well-used expression of her mother's that she'd just remembered. She was seeing both Choker and Knox at different times: meeting the poet in the city or the outskirts of Shipden to be taken for drinks, meals and sexual adventures, and also on other nights inviting her neighbour to supper in her flat while he, in turn, occasionally took her to the cinema or for local Chinese or Indian meals. He had a huge amount of course work to get through and didn't allow himself much time off.

She found Knox easy. He laughed a great deal, often at himself, in contrast to Choker who took himself very seriously. Choker liked to have long debates with Eve about who was the most significant post-war poet. She found the intellectual work of some poets too cryptically inaccessible for her taste and much preferred to discuss his work that he'd given her to read. He was forever declaring his need to write with 'stylistic integrity'. She kept quiet much of the time and listened to his monologues.

So far, Knox didn't pry into her past and didn't ask what she was doing when she wasn't with him. Increasingly she found herself drawn to him.

While their relationship was platonic, more and more they looked at each other with sexual interest. She wanted to touch those lobeless ears and that strong jaw, but resisted.

When their days to go to the city coincided, he took her in his VW, which she appreciated, especially when the weather was bad.

Mum. There is quite a good underground train system in central Beijing with two different train lines. One is LINE1 which goes in a straight line and the other is called THE LOOP LINE for obvious reasons. It's marvellously straightforward, nothing like the complicated Tokyo train system that had me frothing at the mouth. When I climb on a train here the whole carriage of passengers turns round and has a good look, which always makes me giggle, so I like to strike a suitable pose, and if they're all really extra interested I do a slow twirl. The Chinese don't really smile, many appear to be quite surly, so I don't think they see the funny side. But most of the ladies who take tickets at the stations like to practise their English and will smile at me if I give them a huge cheesy grin. Visited Tiananmen Square and The Forbidden City. The buildings and architecture are great and I had a good time ambling round. I've been walking the Wall. It was exhausting as it is up and down steep steps that have often worn away completely, which is a bit of a worry. Great chunks of wall are missing with huge drops, so when I'd reached the stage of having wobbly jelly legs from going up and down I had to concentrate. Mind you it was worth it as the views are breath-taking, you can see for miles and miles over China and Mongolia over the mountains. I walked with a Japanese girl called Suzuki and we were both completely crumped by the end of it. She was sleeping in the bunk above me in the hostel dorm and snoring a split second before I zonked out into a deep slumber. I woke the next morning and had no idea where I was at all. I looked around for a full five minutes wondering what all the people in bunk beds were doing. Very mysterious and it hasn't happened very often so far, which is surprising considering the amount of different places I've slept in over the months. I haven't seen my Australian friend for a while, but expect to meet him again next month. His name is Russell and he's tall but not huge. Best be off, the Chinese internet access is slow and it takes forever to send a message. Love from Wobbly Legs. Xxx

Jez. Hope your legs are recovering from the Great Wall. It sounds a punishing experience. How do you find authentic Chinese food? I imagine that it's not much like the stuff we get from Chinese takeaways here. There's a new one opened very near the flat and it's good, vast amounts for small sums. I have a new neighbour here who is a really good guy. He's called Knox Smith. Very likeable. He drives me around, which is great in this horrible weather. You need warm clothes out there. I miss you. Love M. xx

For the first time it was cold enough in Shipden for Eve to wear an ancient sheepskin hat and knitted scarf. At the Post Office she met Hester togged out in a long, emerald velvet cloak and hood.

'You look like a character from a fairy tale!' Eve grinned.

'Hopefully not one of Grimms.'

'No. More one of Charles Perrault's. Cinderella's fairy godmother,' said Eve, lying.

'Let's go next door for a hot drink. I'm frozen and I need to tell you something.' Hester led the way into the Viennese cafe.

They settled at a window table and ordered coffee.

Hester carefully removed her outer wrappings and folded them on a chair. 'It's terribly sad. It's about poor Amos. I just met the ironmonger on the High Street. And he told me.'

Oh, no, thought Eve, what's coming now? 'I haven't seen our neighbour for ages,' she said.

Hester told her how Amos had gone off alone on holiday, then, according to his boss, suffered some sort of nervous breakdown and been sent to a psychiatric hospital for treatment. 'I feel guilty, as I'd never even noticed he wasn't around. But I've been busy and not always at home. Anyway…' Hester pushed a hanging curtain of black hair behind one ear. "This is just awful. Apparently, Amos left the hospital yesterday without being discharged. He just walked out and came back to Shipden on the bus. He must have been in a really bad way, because he climbed the church tower. You know he'd never done that before, being so unfit.'

Eve imagined the fat man struggling up the stone steps, gasping and wheezing in the confined space.

'Well, he got to the top and it must have taken him forever.' Hester gripped the edge of the table and stared at her knuckles. There was a long silence. She raised her head. 'Then he threw himself off.'

'Oh, God.' Eve shivered, full of pity. Is this all my fault? she thought. Did he do that because of me? She stared out through the window at the grey bulk of the church and its huge, traceried windows. She craned her neck to see the battlements and pinnacles above. The tallest tower in Norfolk, so very high. Then down to the surrounding grass. She imagined him despairing, giving up on his lonely life and falling, an unwieldy dark boulder, from the colourless sky.

'The people from the shoe shop found him.' Hester blew her nose. 'The poor man apparently met an excitable woman called Keziah in hospital. She was a patient too, and she led him on for ages, teasing him. He thought she really felt affection for him and he got all worked up and asked her to marry him. Then she just laughed at him and ridiculed him in front of everyone. Told him he was the ugliest and stupidest man she'd ever met.'

'No!' Eve could think of nothing to say.

'He had a long history of relationships that never happened. One rejection after another.' She sighed. 'The ironmonger's going to organise a funeral. Amos didn't have any family left here. But he lived in the town all his life and there are lots of people who knew him.'

'We'll all go from Strand House. I'm so sorry. What a terrible thing to happen.'

'I only wish I'd been kinder to him. I always knew he was a bit...' Hester paused. 'Odd is the word I'm searching for. One shouldn't speak ill of the dead. But he could be troublesome.'

Eve remembered the horrible evening in his company

which she had relived many times. 'I know,' she said, fumbling with a tissue in her pocket. 'But no one should die like that.'

Sometime after the funeral, the evening of the Shipden Christmas lights switch-on turned out wet and cold. Eve and Knox, full of his homemade *gluhwein*, stood in the drizzle with a crowd of local people and clapped Father Christmas who sat, ho-hoing and making his festive speech on a dais in front of the church. As the lights went on, magically the rain stopped.

Eve tucked her chilly arm in Knox's and they wandered the streets, investigating the colourful stalls of arts and crafts, and watching the screaming, laughing children riding the roundabouts. Hurdy-gurdy music filled the open space. Infants in woolly hats gazed at the lights and large decorated tree with round eyes. Eve looked at them and remembered Jez at three, her excitement at visiting Santa in his grotto.

'You seem sad. What's the matter?' Knox bent towards her.

'I'm missing my daughter. I wish she could be with me for Christmas.'

He stared at her. 'All this time I've known you and you never said you had children.'

'You never asked. Anyway, just one. Not a child any more. She's on the other side of the world.'

'Youngsters have to do their own thing.' He watched a small, pink-cheeked girl dressed in a furry panda suit as she consumed a cloud of candyfloss. 'I'd like to have children.'

She glanced at him in surprise, but said nothing.

As they passed an open pub doorway, heat, faint music, and a scent of cinnamon and beer flooded out. 'Let's go in here,' he invited.

They settled in a dark corner with their drinks and stared around at the red-painted walls, holly decorations and open fire burning aromatic logs.

'You must have had your daughter very young,' he said. 'You only look in your twenties now.'

She laughed. 'I was a teenager. It's not so easy being a mother. I could see my own mother's point of view for the first time.'

'What's she like?'

Eve had warmed to Knox even more that evening. For the first time she talked willingly and didn't change the subject.

'My mother? She's not around anymore. Had quite a hard time. She was born in the war, the child of an American GI. Her mother didn't want her so she was sent to live in various children's homes in north London and Essex. As she grew up, she turned out to be very insecure, wanting affection and not getting it and then falling into trouble as a result, as far as I understand. Not having any family of her own, or knowing where her mother could be, must have been awful.' Eve rubbed her eyes. 'She once told me that she felt she never had anybody. No one showed interest in her. As an adult she had various jobs, she was working as an artist's model when she became pregnant with me.' Eve drained her glass and stared into the fire.

'She must have been attractive.'

'She was, but men took advantage of her, I think. She couldn't look after me well. Didn't know how, I suppose, so I was in foster care a lot. The times I spent with her were good, on the whole. But she went off the rails and ended up in prison.' Eve felt an ache in her throat but managed to smile at Knox. 'Basically, she didn't deserve the hard life she had. She looked after me when she could. The best spell for me came when as a teenager; I lived off and on with a foster family south of London. They encouraged me with my education and I began to read for pleasure. They took me to art galleries and museums. If it hadn't been for them, I'd never in a million years been able to study when I had the chance later. Thanks to them I had all sorts of jobs and got an Arts degree.' Eve, aware that she had never before said so much about her past, felt dizzy and strangely empty. Was this a betrayal of her mother after so long? Should she have kept quiet?

'And your mother now?'

'She died years ago.' Eve remembered how she'd carried the ashes back in a tin from the crematorium. 'She never even saw Jez, who took after her. The same big eyes and wispy hair. But my mother was more fine-boned. Had delicate hands like a child.'

'You must miss her. Can I ask why she was in prison?'

'I don't want to talk about her any more now.'

'Did you know who your father was?' he persisted.

'No.' Eve wanted to change the subject. She studied Knox's familiar, slightly flaring nostrils, the curiosity was raw in his eyes. 'Your parents are both—dead.'

'That's right. I've no other family.'

'What are you doing for Christmas? Going away?'

'No. I'm just going to hibernate in Shipden. I've various business plans to write and solutions to case studies. A pile of work. Very time-consuming. You?'

'I'll be here. It'll be quiet. Hester, the Tomblings and Cheryl and Troy will all be somewhere else. Hester's going to her son's.'

'Excellent. We can be riotous, play loud music and get blasted on the day. If I buy the turkey and all the festive stuff, will you cook it? We can have Christmas together.' He grinned.

'There's nothing I'd like better.' She was delighted. 'I'll get some crackers. We can get a tree. Do things properly.'

Mum. Hope you have a good Christmas. Sorry I can't be there. I'm in India now and it's great, fabulous countryside and amazing architecture. I've been to Delhi and around about. The poverty is terrible though, the villages and towns packed with people sleeping on the streets, clothes in tatters, all trying to scrape a living. They look happy, but I suppose they're used to living like this. Wherever I go I'm besieged by people holding their hands out for money. I just feel so guilty because I don't have bags of cash for everyone. I visited Agra and the Taj Mahal, and Jaipur—the pink city, which is huge and sprawling and I've been on an elephant and a camel. I spent some time in a Rajasthan village eating great curries (I have curd with everything and suffer no ill effects) and watched some women dancing over sharp knives and broken glass. Had my left hand painted with henna and thought it would go well with the red blob on my forehead. But that sadly washed off, although the henna's lasting. It's a large swirly pattern of orange that looks like a hideous skin condition and I recoil in horror when I catch it out of the corner of my eye. I've met up with Russell again. We get on very well and he's looking after me. You'd approve. Much love Jez XX

Jez. I'm so glad you're enjoying yourself. I'll be thinking of you on Christmas Day and remembering all the good ones we spent together. It's good that you're not on your own. Neither am I. Knox and I shall spend the day together. You'd approve too. Love always, M. xxx

The day before Christmas was quiet in Strand House. At her window, Eve watched Hester, the last occupant, apart from Knox and herself, to leave the building. As Hester bundled her dogs into the Morris Traveller and drove away, Choker rang. 'Hello, beauty. Wish we could be together tomorrow.'

'But we can't.'

'Very true. But I've a gift in my hot hand. May I come round and spend the evening with you? I'm longing to see you, and your flat. After all this time I've never been chez toi and I'm curious to view your nest.'

She paused at the thought of Choker and Knox meeting on the stairs or of Knox hearing Choker through the thin wall between their flats. 'Your curiosity will have to wait. But I'll meet you at the Dragon in a bit.'

'I see. You have a lover at home already?'

'Heaps of them.' She giggled.

'This isn't the brush off, then?'

'No. See you at eight.'

The night was terrible. A gale-force blew up. As Eve struggled along the promenade hearing the lashing waves thunder on the other side of the wall, she remembered that the ferocious seas round that part of the coast had caused the area to be known as The Devil's Throat. There had been many shipwrecks in the past. A howling darkness surrounded her. She hurried up the steps, clinging to the cold handrail.

The distinctive Chakour vehicle was parked outside the Dragon. As she approached cautiously, fearing that Venetia might be inside, the driver's window wound down and Choker's head appeared. 'Going my way, lady?'

She settled in the front passenger seat and thawed out. 'I'm not sure about the lady bit.'

The car moved swiftly off. Choker laughed. 'You do look very wild.'

'There's a hurricane, in case you hadn't noticed.'

He took his hand from the wheel and smoothed her scrambled hair. 'Very Medusa.' They whistled down the little streets and out into the country. 'I've the key to a friend's house. He's away just now. We can make ourselves comfortable.'

The sun shone and the wind dropped on Christmas Day. Eve stared out of her window at the gleaming waves rolling to the shore. She fingered the elaborate antique gold necklace that Choker had given her the night before. He'd fastened it for her and she'd wished she had something more exciting to give him than the small oil painting of Shipden pier she'd done.

He scrutinised the signature. 'Brilliant.'

She wasn't sure whether he was praising her painting or showing pleasure that she had put her initials rather than her full name on it.

'I'll hang it in my study. It's really excellent.'

Nothing more was said.

Slowly she unfastened the necklace, which felt warm from being next to her throat all night, and put it in her jewellery box. She didn't want Knox to see her wearing it.

Taking the turkey from her fridge she prepared it with onions, butter and chestnut stuffing and put it in the oven. Her thumbnails hurt from peeling the chestnuts.

As she towelled herself after showering, she heard Knox through the wall singing in his bathroom. She smiled and put on her best dress, a long lilac velvet one she'd had for some time.

The day turned out to be a good one. She and Knox hardly stopped laughing from the moment he came in, wearing a Father Christmas outfit and red toe socks, and carrying a pillowcase of odd presents for her. There were wrapped parsnips (her favourite vegetable), the holey beach stones that she collected, chocolate angels, soaps shaped like slugs, bottles of bath bubbles, games for two players, exotically scented candles and books of jokes. She was touched he had taken so much trouble.

'I'm afraid I only have one thing for you.' She gave him her elaborately wrapped gift.

He untied the gauze ribbon. 'A painting of the lighthouse. How interesting that you give me this phallic symbol. A meaningful present.' He winked.

She laughed. 'I never saw it like that. I just hoped it would be recognisable.'

'Did you paint it?'

She nodded.

He looked at her in admiration. 'I'm very impressed. It really is good. Not a photographic likeness, there's something of you in this, but I can't explain. I'm not at all arty-farty.' He gazed around him as if for the first time. 'Now I can see that all these paintings on your walls have the same technique. I knew you were a painter but I never really thought about it at all. You're so clever.'

She burned with pleasure.

January

Mum. Happy New Year! I've just had a great fortnight with Russell. We visited the holy town of Pushkar and stayed in a palace hotel on the edge of the lake. We went to one of the 500 temples around the lake and had to throw a pile of flowers into the water at the same time as different chanting. Very complicated and we're not sure what it was about, but I have a piece of red string tied round my wrist by a priest to show that I've done it. We also stayed in two great forts that are now hotels, full of huge murals and vast pieces of antique furniture, and enormous bathrooms with marble floors. Acoustics good for singing. Russell is tone deaf but sings along to tapes of Hindu and Rajasthan desert music in the hire car. With windows open we hurtle along singing loudly. People stare at us as we go through villages, just to find out what the racket is. I especially like the desert music of a man doing a kind of grumbling yodelling noise and Russell has given me this tape for Christmas. Lots of musical love, Jez XXX

Jez. Happy New Year to you, too! Your Christmas sounds special. I had a great time with Knox. He has a good sense of humour and keeps me laughing. He insisted that we watch all the old classic Monty Python and Yes, Prime Minister videos, his favourites, not mine. Very relaxing. Particularly since we just sat around for a week eating and drinking solidly. We hardly left the house and our friendship is thoroughly bonded. I have, however, put on a great deal of weight. Lots of fat love M. XXX

Hester came back from her holiday full of excitement about her manuscript, My Life With Hugo.

'Eve, it's bloody brilliant! Choker found me an agent who's found me a publisher. Can you imagine, they want to publish it this year? Hugo would be so chuffed. The old devil. His writing was so witty and he was really popular not so long ago. It'll bring him back into the public eye.'

'And you, too, Hester.' Eve hugged her. 'Congratulations. You deserve it.'

'They're talking about money, too. I'd no idea. I'll be up and down to London like a yo-yo soon. Of course, I've Choker to thank for all his help.'

'How is he?' Eve hadn't seen him since Christmas Eve.

'Oddly enough, he's a bit down. Not like him at all. Apparently, he hasn't written a thing himself for weeks. He mumbles about writer's block, but I don't believe in such a thing. He seems plagued by self-doubt; says he can't do it anymore. It's a failure of confidence. But I've never known him like this before.'

'Perhaps he's having a hard time with Venetia.' What a bitch I am, thought Eve.

'His married life doesn't usually have the slightest effect on his writing,' Hester said acidly. 'Still, he has plenty of reviewing to keep him busy. I've no doubt the muse hasn't forsaken him entirely. He'll get back to writing in due course. His last collection only came out just before Christmas.'

'I didn't know that. What's it called?'

'*Girl in a Tower*. No doubt some sort of metaphor. I couldn't understand half the poems. Very inaccessible I thought. But he always gets good reviews.'

Is it about me? Eve wondered, half proud, half fearful. I must get a copy. Why didn't he tell me about it?

The College term was well underway and she walked through the crowded city in her lunch hour to find a bookshop. The sales were still on and throngs of women with huge carrier bags moved slowly down the pavements.

In the distance, crossing the street, she saw Cheryl with her bright copper hair, pushing Troy in the buggy. But what was so surprising, what caused her to stop abruptly, was the fact that Choker walked with Cheryl, his arm around her shoulder. As Eve stared in amazement at his familiarity, the trio stopped too, and Choker leaned over and gave Cheryl a passionate kiss on the mouth.

I must be mistaken, Eve thought, it can't be Choker. She went nearer. But it was him, in his usual worn leather jacket.

None of them saw her in the crush. She just gazed at them.

Despite the cold Cheryl wore skin-tight jeans and a cropped top and had regained her thin figure, no longer appearing pregnant, white-faced and sick. The girl with the short upper lip and the long legs smiled and her young skin shone.

Eve remembered seeing Choker and Cheryl talking together outside Strand House at times, and in Hester's flat. There had been no apparent intimacy, no flirting, no staring in each other's eyes. But perhaps they had just been careful.

Once they disappeared round a corner, Eve slumped on a bench. So that's the way it is, she thought. He must think I'm a fool. Well, I was an idiot to assume I was the only one. He's probably sleeping with all the women in Strand House except Grace. She felt heat flood her face. That's it. The end. Never again. She strode back to the College in a rage, forgetting to do her shopping.

All afternoon, as she attempted to teach her students about Cubism, to talk about the intellectual conception of form and colour and the combination of several views of a subject all more or less superimposed, she saw snapshots of Choker and Cheryl with their heads together at various angles.

That evening at Knox's suggestion she waited for him at the University to give her a lift back to Shipden. Cold and disturbed, she wandered up and down outside the buildings in the dark. Under the streetlights she recognised places, but they seemed strangely altered at night.

Everything was a negative. All that should be black was

white and vice versa. The daytime solid black-branched trees had transformed into foreign pale columns and arches, intricate patterns of white lace fluttering against the darkness, moving and sighing in the wind. The scent of rain came out of the shadows along wet gutters and glittering mosaics of tarmac. It curled around drainpipes and dripping leaves. Two tall chimneys like blanched willows pumped pale feathers of smoke to drift and disperse over the pin-pricked sky. Windows seemed squares of blankness in white cubes. Young voices echoed down shrouded paths as pallid figures, beaded with moisture, slipped between the ghostly trees like spies.

She turned up her coat collar against the damp wind, the strangeness, the youngsters and the waiting.

Eventually Knox came running down the road. 'Here you are.' He hugged her for the first time. 'I'm so sorry to be so long. The lecture went on and on and I couldn't get away.'

'That's all right. It's good to have a lift home.' They walked towards the car park.

'You look tragic. Is everything okay?' He stopped to catch his breath.

'I'm fine.' But she still churned with anger and emptiness.

In his camper van driving north, they didn't speak. She was aware that normally they chattered and laughed all the way, so she felt gratitude to him for not pushing her to explain.

She glanced at him as they passed the Shipden sign. His profile lit up against the darkness looked stern. His chin determined, his back so straight. He's worth more than anyone I know, she thought. I deserve this man. Not Choker, not a cheat.

As they climbed the stairs, she caught his hand. 'Knox, I'm sorry. I was just cold and in a bad mood. Thank you for putting up with me. Give me ten minutes to have a bath and thaw out, then come and have a drink in my flat. I've a couple of bottles of Rioja that have been hanging around too long.'

He stopped outside Cheryl's door and ran his hand over his chin. 'I'll get rid of my stubble. Yes, that's the best invitation I've had all week. Neither of us needs to be up at sparrowfart for work. I'll see you shortly.'

While hot water ran in the bathroom, Eve lit his scented candles in her bedroom, straightened the crimson Indian cotton hangings and bedcover there and put slow jazz music on, opened her wine, found two large glasses, then stepped with cold feet into the steaming bath. Nervous and excited, she recalled the expression in Knox's eyes. He'd known what she meant. The time at last was right.

She woke early, conscious of someone breathing beside her. Dim pink light through the curtains showed Knox sleeping soundly, half-smiling and warm, hair curling on his naked chest and arms. Aware of a certain happiness, she watched him sleep for a while.

He stirred and ran a hand over her body, stroking her bare thigh. Then sighed and fell deeply asleep again.

She knew all she wanted was to wake beside him every morning and to look after him. Creeping out of bed, she decided to go for a run while he slept. She felt full of new energy. She pulled on an old tracksuit, then quietly left the flat.

Cold air cut into her face as she stepped out of the front door. She'd not known it so chilly before in Shipden.

'We rarely get frost here,' Hester had said once.

But the wall and road ahead glistened with a white tinsel. Shivering, she jogged slowly, puffing cloudy breath, feeling her head thumping, towards the sea.

She paused at the little boating pond on the cliff and almost turned round, thinking about Knox, thinking the winter chill was a punishment she didn't need.

The pool had frozen over in the night and some passer-by

had recently smashed the ice. Mirror-like fragments lay around and where the water was exposed gulls drank and splashed noisily.

The bright sun low in the sky was dazzling, so she didn't hear or see someone come up behind her. The person put cold hands over her eyes.

At once she struggled, frightened. Her heart beat like a jackhammer behind her ribs.

'Guess who?'

A familiar voice.

She turned. 'That's not funny, Choker.'

'Sorry. You're running bright and early.'

'And you, what are you doing?'

'Just wandering. I don't believe in exercise, as you know. Come with me and we'll have breakfast somewhere. A big fry-up.'

'No, thanks. I don't have time.' She looked him in the eye. 'I saw you with Cheryl in the city yesterday.'

'You should have joined us. Cheryl's lovely but she has no conversation.' His heavy-lidded eyes were sly.

'She appears to have lost her baby.'

For the first time she'd known him he looked crushed, his confidence diminished. 'Don't talk about it,' he murmured.

'There's no one around to hear.'

'I just helped her out, that's all. Anyway, it's none of your business.' He stamped some ice underfoot. 'I knew her long before I met you.'

'I see.' The pain round her forehead increased its grip. 'I've decided I don't want to meet you again.' She saw how the bright light exposed wrinkles round his mouth. 'We had fun, but it's over. I'll give you the necklace back and the ear rings.'

'No need. Keep them as tokens of my affection.' He touched her cold cheek. 'You may change your mind. And forget about Cheryl. She's nothing to me. I only slept with her when I was drunk. A pretty young girl available. You know how these things are, Eve. You understand. You've lived a bit. Don't be hurt.' He sighed. 'I'll get back to you. I admire your talent so much. You're a generous, affectionate woman. Our affair actually meant something to me.'

She remembered that she'd never wanted an intense loving relationship with Choker, but because he'd been such a skilled lover there had been times when she'd ached with need for him. She'd learned to care for him. Hadn't she?

'And me,' she admitted. 'But it's over now.' She shook his hand free of her shoulder and ran, stiff-backed down the avenue to Strand House.

February

Mum. I'm loving India but I'm not sure if you will ever get this message as internet access here is difficult. The roads are terrible, packed with traffic including buses laden with people hanging out of windows, off the sides and piled on the roof. They sometimes run into low-hanging electric cables with hideous results. Of course the roads are also full of cows, goats and pigs ambling along. The noise of honking horns and squealing brakes is appalling. The other day the car in front of Russell and me just veered off the road and ended up on its side in the ditch. As we went to help a tribe of people climbed out of the window. Incredibly no one had any broken bones. I think because they'd all been asleep, including the driver, and were so squashed they didn't fly around inside the car. Only one woman was cut badly, so I found the first aid kit you gave me and used the antiseptic wipes and bandages. Then I talked to a man with an enormous moustache and neatly combed beard who said he'd spent a lovely afternoon with his friends smoking an opium pipe. He invited me to try, but I politely declined. A very nice lady showed me how to wear a sari. I said goodbye to Russell as he's gone back to Australia, and caught a night train at Kota. All the children in the compartment had fun trooping past me and staring. When I spoke to them they burst into giggles and scuttled off. Am in Bombay now.
Much love, Jez XXX

Jez. There's snow here but it probably won't last. I've been thinking of you and remembering that snowman we made in Brighton. The snowman with two faces, nice and nasty. And how we went sledging with Mrs Priest's best tray. How furious she was! It's so cold. The wind whipped up huge waves yesterday. They came crashing over the walls on the front and threw pebbles and sand all over. My part-time teaching has been cut down a bit. I'm happy about it as it gives me more time to paint and I can sell *my stuff to the hotels. People are getting used to me in Shipden now, I'm quite at home. There are snowdrops and aconites in the flowerbeds and one rosebush, in a sheltered place, has flowered all winter. No doubt it's due for a heavy prune soon. I haven't seen Vernon in the garden for ages. Must away. Much love, M. XXX*

Eve turned the computer off and stared out of the window. Grace was struggling up the street with bags of shopping. The pavement looked slippery and messy with snow and the old lady tapped hesitantly with her stick.

At once Eve ran downstairs to help her.

'Take my arm and I'll carry these bags. It's not a good day to be out.'

Grace's turquoise woolly hat was dusted white. 'Thank you so much, Eve. I know. It's horrible. But I had to fetch Vernon's medicine so I thought I'd do the shopping too.' Her gentle, mournful face quivered.

'What's the matter with him?'

'He has pleurisy. On antibiotics. He's always been chesty, poor Vernon. But he's in quite a bad way.' She climbed the step with difficulty. 'Our daughter in the country wants us to live with her. She and her husband have a room for us downstairs. And there's a big garden. Days like today I think it would be a good idea. I'm needing a hip replacement.'

Eve carried the bags into the Tomblings' home. 'I'm sorry. Let me do your shopping for you, please? I'm always nipping in and out for things so it'll be no trouble. Just let me know when you need something.'

She ran upstairs. As she passed the 'A.Postle' flat she heard banging inside. So it's been sold already, she thought. Three days earlier two scruffy youths with a local removal van had emptied the rooms of their beige furniture. I hope it's nobody very young moving in, she wished. Although I don't mind hearing washing machines and loud telephone conversations, I'm not always keen on other people's taste in music. Knox and the Tomblings, above and below Cheryl, complained about her rock music played at full volume late at night and in the early hours.

Glancing from her window again, she noted that birds' claw prints in the pristine snow on the garden pointed like arrows towards the sea. Rooftops shone white or black depending on the thaw and the warmth from the house. Gulls perched morosely on chimneys in front of a metallic sky leached of colour. Everything was depicted in shades of black, white or grey.

Eve propped her latest canvas on the easel and prepared to paint.

A few minutes later someone heavily banged the brass knocker on her flat door.

That's not Knox or Hester, she thought. Too aggressive. She put down her palette knife and went to see. She was taken aback to find Venetia Chakour, red-faced and out of breath on the landing.

'Mrs Tombling told me you lived here.' She barged straight past Eve without waiting to be invited and stormed into the living room, her head wagging from side to side as she seemed to be searching the small area. 'Is my husband here?'

'No.' Eve was shocked at the way her home was invaded. She made herself speak slowly. 'Your husband is not here now and never has been here. Why do you imagine he might be?'

Venetia flushed even more. Her snail nose twitched. She turned round without answering and pushed into the remaining rooms of the flat.

'Make yourself at home. Look under the bed, why don't you?' Eve followed her. 'What about in here? See? Nothing.' She helpfully opened her hall cupboard to reveal her tatty old coat and scratched vacuum cleaner. 'I'd like to get on with my painting now if you've finished.'

'Marc's disappeared.' Venetia faced her, protuberant eyes blinking. 'I assumed you would know where he is.'

For a moment Eve almost pitied her. 'Well, I don't. As I understand it, he's prone to disappearing. No doubt he'll turn up.' She looked out of the window to see if his motorbike was parked round the side. It wasn't. 'If you'll excuse me, I must get on.'

Venetia's lips tightened. 'I know all about you,' she shouted. 'Whore!' She pushed past onto the landing and slammed the door behind her.

Eve subsided on her sofa bed. She badly needed a cigarette, although it was a long time since she'd stopped smoking. With some fascination she watched her own hand shake.

A gentle tap on her door.

She ignored it.

The tap persisted.

Cautiously she opened her door. Knox stood there. He appeared concerned. 'Are you all right? Who the hell was that shouting?'

'You've heard Hester talk about her poet friend, Choker, who helps her with her writing. That was his wife. She's lost him.'

Knox peered over the banisters. 'She's beating on Hester's door now. Poor thing. She sounds disturbed.'

'She is. She used to advise old Amos. But she has right on her side.'

'Really? I pity her husband. On the subject of Amos, though, I've something to show you. I want your advice. Forget about that ranting woman.' He led her downstairs to the first floor and, taking a key from his pocket, unlocked Amos's flat door, directly below hers.

'What are you doing, Knox? Where did you get that key from?'

'Don't sound so worried. The flat's mine. I bought it with

my inheritance. Dead cheap, too. No mod cons.' He tapped his chest with pride.

She didn't like to ask him why. Certainly, his own place was tiny. Reluctantly she followed him, remembering the last time she'd been there. But on this occasion, it felt different, the living room was an empty shell, the orange daisy curtains had been thrown away and snowy light flooded through the great bay window. 'It was you banging about in here, cleaning.'

'Yup. This is going to be my bedroom and this little room a dressing room. I'm going to completely redo the kitchen and bathroom. Just turn them into one decent sized bathroom. Shall I have a jacuzzi?'

She laughed. 'What about your place upstairs?'

'I'll carry on living up there, cooking and so on. I'm just going to sleep down here. With you, of course. It's going to be fantastic. I've bought a fabulous bed at an auction. It'll come later. It's antique, Victorian. Huge, brass and steel, decorated with balls and hearts. The sex in it will be magnificent. I'll get a new, vast mattress. It's to entice you down out of your red room.'

'Don't you like my romantic bedroom?'

'Of course. Don't look so offended. I've had the best time of my life there. It's just that I want us to create this together. I admire your taste so much.'

'How are you going to pay for all this?'

'Good question, since I was an impoverished student until recently.' He blew his nose on a scarlet handkerchief. 'Do you remember my father died, before you and I met properly? He left everything to me. I'm the only survivor in my family. I've sold his house in Scotland and the money's coming through now. I have a master plan concerning this house.' He spread out his arms. 'Isn't this room great? What colour scheme shall we have?'

There wasn't a second's hesitation. 'Terracotta, gold and

white, with a pale marble fireplace to burn logs. We can search the reclamation places for it. Antique gilded mirrors. A chandelier up there.' She glanced at the high ceiling. 'And a gold and white bathroom. All classical designs. We can choose the tiles in the city.'

'You bet.' He clutched her and they danced round and round the cold room, their shoes clacking on the floorboards.

'Hester will wonder what on earth's going on. She'll be tapping on the ceiling, setting her dogs on us.' She gasped, kissed him, and disengaging herself, leaned against the windowsill in time to see Venetia's car move out of the drive and join the traffic. 'A magic bed,' she murmured. 'And huge, fluffy, white towels. The very height of luxury. Imagine it.'

The weather threw blizzards. On the coast unused crab boats were pulled high out of reach of the angry sea vomiting up spray. Inland, it was worse, with snow blocking roads and rural electricity supplies cut off.

'I'm going to stay at the University a few days,' Knox told Eve. 'The forecast's bad and I've a lot on I can't afford to miss. So I'm taking my sleeping bag and staying over at Dave's. He's on my course. Bloke with the ginger moustache.'

'I remember. Tweed jacket man.' Eve washed the mugs. 'I'm lucky I don't have to go to work at all until next week. I have my essays to mark here. I'll stay in the warm. But I'll miss you.' She kissed his cold ear. 'Take care in the camper.'

'I'll miss you, too. The builder for downstairs is supposed to be coming tomorrow. Here's the key to number four. You're OC now.'

'What's that?'

'Officer in charge.'

'Great.'

'I'll ring you when I can.'

After he'd gone, Eve shopped for Grace and took a flowering

azalea to Vernon who still lay in bed but felt stronger.

She went to see Hester who poured her a cup of excessively strong coffee.

'Did you see Venetia the other day?' asked Eve. 'She called on me.'

Hester snorted. 'Thankfully I was out when she came round. Uninvited. But she rang me. Blessed Choker's gone missing again. If she can't keep her man that's her fault. She threatened to divorce him, this time, and one can't blame her.' She patted the labradors at her feet. 'But he's becoming known now and earning more with his reviews and newspaper column, so I suppose he can afford to leave her.' The dog with the grey muzzle looked up mournfully into her face. 'Poor boy. I'm more concerned about this dear creature. I'm going to take him to the vet later. He's not at all well. Getting old.' Lighting a cigarette, she stared up at the dog portrait. 'You did a good job, Eve, my love. If I have to have the poor old bugger put down, I'll always have this to remember him by.' Her eyes, screwed up in the smoke, looked suspiciously damp.

Eve, despondent, slowly climbed the stairs to her flat. She didn't want to be parted from Knox and kept imagining him, his strong chin, the loving look in his eyes.

She sighed. Tomorrow's my birthday, she thought, and no one knows. I don't want to tell anyone here. I'd have mentioned it to Knox but he'd have felt he'd have to come back to be with me. Anyway, I don't want to celebrate. There are reasons to be melancholy. I'll just get through it on my own.

The next evening, as she walked on the chilly beach in the winter dusk, watching the colours of land, sea and sky drain out in the smoky half-light, she thought of the last time she'd seen Jez.

Then she saw at the water's edge, lying half buried in the

sand, a skull. One black eye socket glared at her as she approached in the twilight. She hesitated, heart pounding, and forced herself nearer. It turned out to be a large flint stone, uncannily like a bony human head. A wave washed over it and it was gone, hidden under water. She shivered and turned to go home.

In the town she bought a Chinese takeaway and sat to eat it in her unlit kitchen, watching cars and solitary people from her window as darkness fell.

The prawns and noodles had no taste. She forced herself to swallow two bites then threw the rest in her rubbish bin. Opening a bottle of Beaujolais, she drank a full glass straight off.

Again, she could hardly taste it. She was unaware of her tears until one fell on her hand.

Her landline rang. She hurried to answer. Thank God for Knox.

But it wasn't. 'Happy birthday, Evey darling!'

'Leo.'

'You don't sound pleased to hear my voice.'

'I haven't heard from you since June. Anyway, after you'd gone I missed my sapphire ring.'

'Oh, that.' The silence lasted half a minute. 'I'm sorry about that. I'd forgotten all about it.'

'Do you have it?'

'Not any more. I had to sell it. I needed the money. Really badly. You understand how it is. You must forgive me, Eve.'

'You don't need to act a part with me, Leo. You're a shit and I can't forgive you.'

'I promise I'll buy you another one just the same. I'm going to be in a porn movie. No kidding. A man I know asked for me specially. I'll be quids in. I'll get you one even better.'

'I don't want anything better. I want my old one back. It was the only thing I had of my mother's. The only thing she had to give me. It meant a lot to me.'

'From what I remember you said about your ma, she sounded a real bitch. I wouldn't have thought you wanted anything to remember her by.'

'That's not for you to judge. I'm going to hang up now,' she shouted.

'No, please don't, sweetie. I'm really sorry. I rang because I know it's a bad time for you. I found your number and I was going to send you flowers, but it was too late for today.'

She put the phone down on the table and poured herself more wine. Drinking it, she could hear his tinny voice issuing from the receiver. 'I was remembering Jez,' he said.

With the gentlest touch she replaced the phone. Then she pulled the wire from its socket so he couldn't call her back.

Bile rose in her throat. She stumbled into the kitchen and vomited in the sink. Turning the tap on, she heard the water rushing but couldn't see it in the darkness. She swilled her mouth out, stopped the tap, lit a candle and opened another bottle of wine. Her heart bumped unevenly in her chest.

The old nightmare was repeating. The pain of her thirty-first. Until then it had always been a day to celebrate. Even if there were only two of them to mark it, herself and Jez, with balloons and cake and ice cream, and a big handmade card from Jez of brilliant-coloured flowers and birds and hearts and a hundred kisses. Eve staggered to the drawer where she kept all the cards Jez had ever made for her. But in her weakened state the drawer was too hard to open and after a few attempts Eve gave up. She drank more wine and lay on the floor and fell asleep.

Later, when she woke, she lit a couple more candles. The electric light would be too harsh. She pulled herself up to her computer and turned it on. Leaning back against the seat, she pressed her palms into her eyes.

New message. She tapped the letters slowly on her keyboard. Her head felt silted up. All her thoughts muddied and spoiled. She unclenched her fists.

Mum. I am missing you so much. I wish you could be here with me.

It was so awful, so difficult to write, to find the letters, to know what to say. What was there to say? It had all been said before. And nothing made the pain go. The terrible loss. What had been hers now gone forever.

She just sat with her head bowed and let tears pour down her face and drip on the keyboard.

There came footsteps on the stairs and a tap on her door.

Go away, she thought. I have to be on my own.

Then she heard Knox's voice. 'Eve. Are you there? Are you all right?'

Slowly she dragged herself to the door and opened it.

'What are you doing in the dark?' He snapped on the light. 'Now I can see you.'

'Don't.' She held her hands over her eyes.

He gripped her shoulders. 'I tried to ring, but the landline seems to be down and your mobile is off. The weather's improved so I decided to come back. I missed you too much.'

Leaning against him, she gave way to choking sobs.

'What's the matter? What is it?' He hugged her close until her crying subsided. 'Come in here.' He helped her into the living room and onto the sofa bed.

Turning on her lamps he went to her computer. 'You've a message from Jez here,' he said. He looked at it more closely. Then he came and sat next to her with his arm around her. 'It's a new message. But from you. It's not from your daughter, is it?'

'No,' she said, her heartbeat racing and palms sweaty. 'I've never had an email from Jez.' She wiped her eyes with a paint rag, smearing burnt umber oil and turpentine down her cheek bone.

'She's not travelling as you said, is she?'

'No. I wanted her just to be on holiday. That's why I

wrote all those emails myself. To make me feel better. To make me feel she's still within reach.'

'I understand.' He stroked her hair back from her face.

'No, you don't. No one can. I just can't bear it that she's dead. That I can't talk to her anymore.' She sobbed again. 'Jez was all I had. We were so happy together. Just the two of us. She was all mine and I knew what she was thinking usually.'

'How did it happen?'

But she stuttered incoherently. 'I-i-it-it…'

'Calm down, Eve,' he coaxed and wiped her eyes.

She shivered and became still. 'Jez was only twelve and it was my birthday. It seems so long ago. We were going out to supper. To celebrate. She chose an Italian place and I had my treat money to pay for it. On the way there, she saw a school friend on the other side of the road and said, "Hang on. I'll be back in a sec." And she darted across the road. And she was hit by a car. That's all. She died in the ambulance.' Eve shuddered, remembering the reflected lights on the wet road, something dark, the scream of brakes and shouts, someone wailing. That keening person was herself, kneeling in the road with blood on her skirt. Then she recalled picking up Jez's shoulder bag, a tiny square of silver sequins, and finding there was nothing inside. 'So quick. So shocking. One minute we were together. Then I was alone for always. That's why I've been pretending to myself that she's still in the world. It keeps her alive. For me. It's a solace, a comfort. Do you understand why I had to write the emails? I wrote about my own experience because after she'd gone, I had to get away too and I travelled by myself. To the Far East. And India was a good place to go. On and off for years I wrote the emails. In a way it was like writing to my own mother. Because I couldn't talk to her either.' She detached herself from him and began biting her fingers.

'Yes. I understand. I'm so very sorry.' He stood, walked over to her computer and closed it down. 'You're not alone.

You have me now. We can care for each other.' He held her close, rocking her in his arms as she wept again for a long time.

'You know, Eve.' He stroked her hair. 'I'm worried about the extent of your unresolved grief. The way you've been acting out this fantasy about Jez, this pretence you've been maintaining all this time, this lack of acceptance of her death. Perhaps now is the time for you to get some psychiatric help. Or see some sort of counsellor. These sessions can be very useful in coming to terms with situations.'

'No,' she said. 'I don't need any help from strangers. I've written all my troubles out now. It's my way of dealing with problems. We needn't talk about my emails any more. It's over. Finished. I won't do it again. It's served its purpose. And thank you for your concern. It means everything to me to know that I'm not alone tonight.'

The next morning, they lay in bed watching the darkness turn to light. 'Eve,' he said, 'are you awake?'

'Yes.'

'I want you to know something. I'm flawed. Don't ever think I'm a good person, because I'm not. In the Army, in my unit, I was known as…'

'Don't tell me.'

'You don't know what I was going to say.'

'I can guess.'

'No. You don't understand. I was very good at my job. I have an excellent record. I served in the Gulf, in Kosovo in 1999, in Afghanistan in 2001. And in Iraq for instance…'

'Don't. I don't want to know about the killing. You are a good person. The kindest man I've known. I'm the flawed one. Anyway, you and I were different people before. Now is now and it's a new beginning for us. You're going to be a business man in a dark suit and I'm going to be a famous artist who exhibits work in the West End.'

121

He turned over and propped himself up on his elbows. 'We're going to make one hell of a lot of money.' He kissed her throat. 'You're so sweet and soft.' Then he looked at the clock. 'Christ!' He sprang naked out of bed and pulled back a curtain. 'Snow's almost gone. I have to get into gear now. But when I get back tonight, we'll drive along the coast to that massive Edwardian hotel and I'll treat you to the best dinner money can buy round here.'

'Mm.' She rolled over into the warm space he'd vacated. 'Tell you something. You've an incredibly muscular backside. One of the wonders of the modern world.'

'I aim to please.'

Troy was arranging the brass chessmen in rows, his small, orange-stained tongue poking out to aid concentration. Then he resorted them into a long line that wound its way round Eve's easel. 'Soldiers!' he shouted, then knocked them down. 'Boom! Boom! Bikit now.'

Eve obliged with a non-chocolate variety, knowing his habit of wiping his sticky fingers on any handy cushion or drapery.

'Me and Churl going Yarmuff soon.'

'For a visit? That'll be nice.'

'Not visit. Going to live in Dave's house. With Dave and Mee-eet loo-oof.'

'Who's Meat Loaf?'

'Herry dog. He's big. Wiv big teef. I et his dinner but he didn't mind.' Troy crunched his biscuit importantly.

'Is Dave nice?'

'Yuss. More bikit now.'

'Please?'

But Cheryl put her head round the door. 'Thanks for having him, Eve. Sorry I was so long. I got things to fix.'

'I hear you're going to move to Yarmouth.'

'S'right. Me and Troy's going back to live with his Dad.

See how it works this time. He's got a job in a big hotel there. And it's livelier than old Shipden. Dead hole, this.' She scratched her bare stomach. 'Troy's going to a day nursery. And I can get a job in a pub I know anytime. We're going next week. Dave's coming for us. I'll be glad to leave them bloody Tomblings. Always on about "noise" and "DHSS". I get bloody sick of it.'

'Bloody sick of it,' echoed Troy, putting the chessmen back on their board.

Eve stroked the top of his head. 'That's kind of you to do that, Troy. You're very helpful. That chess set belongs to Knox.'

'Knox is cool. Brilliant. Carried the buggy up for me the other day.' With a fluorescent yellow bobble Cheryl arranged her copper coils of hair into a nest on top of her head. 'If he wasn't already just now tied up with you, I'd've invited him to play games with me.'

'Thanks for holding back then.'

Cheryl cackled as she took Troy downstairs.

March

'Tell me about Jez.'

'I'm always talking about her. You must have heard everything by now.' Eve stopped at a patch of saffron crocuses and white hyacinths in the cliff gardens. 'Look at these. It must be Spring already.' Her nose felt stuffy.

'It must. I'm certainly nest building.' With satisfaction Knox watched a starling flying past with a twig in its beak. 'This time tomorrow flat three will be mine.'

'You own half of Strand House already. Do you want all of it?'

'I certainly do. Hopefully in time the other flats will be available. I can't afford to do them all up yet, but we can sort them out in the next few years. The whole house will just be for us.' He pulled her to him.

Eve's hair blew into her face and hid her smile.

'I only wish I didn't have so much course work,' he continued. 'I should be getting on with my dissertation this very moment, instead of walking in the sun with you. Let's just go to the top of the cliff and back. Anyway, we were talking about Jez.'

'You were.'

'Who was her father? That guy Leo you've mentioned?'

She felt her skin prickling and her mouth filling with the taste of metal. 'No, not him. It was a man I didn't know well and I've not seen since.'

'You mean, he didn't know about her?'

'That's right.' She walked on.

He caught her hand. 'Why didn't you want him to know?'

'I'd already left the area by the time I knew I was pregnant. I didn't want to see him again.' She looked out to sea where the waves calmly rolled in never-ending ripples to the sand. 'He was a priest.' She shivered.

'What!'

In the silence that followed she stared at him, trying to gauge his thoughts.

'Did he take advantage of you?' Knox's hand gripped hers. 'You were very young. Was he one of those...' he hesitated, 'paedophiles?'

Eve thought back, remembering the bony young man in his dark robes, his skin so white, his hollowed cheeks, thin expressive eyebrows and delicate mouth. They were both so skinny, so shy, and he was only a few years older than her after all. 'No, he wasn't. I needed affection and attention, and he was just kind. He didn't know how to send me away. I met him in an art gallery and he bought me a cup of coffee and talked about paintings. We both liked the same artists. He explained things. Told me about triptychs, the Madonna at the centre and patron Saints on the wings, you know. Then when the triptych is shut you can see the owner's coat of arms on the backs of the wings.' She turned her collar up against the breeze and remembered his soft voice. 'I didn't know anything like that. About altarpieces. I'd just gone in out of the cold. Because it was free. Though I really liked some of the paintings.'

'But he took advantage of you,' Knox persisted.

'No. The opposite. After he shook my hand and left, I couldn't bear it. So I followed him home through London. Without him seeing me. He walked for miles. I saw where he went, a building next to a church, and late that night I came back and knocked on his door.' She remembered her hunger, the way he looked when he opened the door, how he invited her into the kitchen, and how, after an hour or so, she slid out of her flimsy clothes and seduced him. 'I initiated it. But afterwards I could see that he felt a terrible guilt. He was shuddering and groaning. He went to pray in the church. So I ran away. I was inexperienced. And it was bad luck to get pregnant.' She turned with her back to the wind. 'Let's go home now. I forgave myself long ago. I think it happened because I didn't have anyone at that time to give a toss about me and I wanted to belong, somehow, to someone. But I knew then he could never belong to me.'

He was really mine, but only for a few minutes, she thought. It was a sort of painful magic, that intimacy. 'After Jez was born, I had someone to care about. And someone to need me. It was fantastic after I had Jez.'

'Did she ask about her father?'

'Not until she was about five. I told her that he'd been a very good man but he'd died. She accepted that quite happily.' Eve looked up into his face. 'I told you I wasn't perfect.'

He smiled down at her. 'No one is. Least of all me.'

When they arrived back at the house, Hester was getting out of her Morris Traveller. She wore dark glasses and her face seemed grey as she stooped wearily to lock the car.

'Are you all right?' asked Eve.

'No, I'm bloody well not.' Hester rubbed her chin. 'I've just had the poor bugger put down. I feel like hell.' She fumbled in her bag.

'Her dog,' mouthed Eve to Knox. Then to Hester, 'I'm so sorry. He was a real character.'

'Here.' Knox put his key in the front door and held it open for them.

'Losing him has helped me make up my mind.' Hester paused outside her flat door. 'I'm taking his brother and going back to live in London again. I still have friends there. I'll miss the long walks on the marshes and beach. But there are other compensations.' She pushed her front door out of her way roughly. 'Now I have every intention of getting drunk.' She disappeared inside as her remaining Labrador barked.

Eve and Knox climbed the stairs. As they passed Cheryl's flat her mother came out carrying a cardboard box of rolled up posters and baby toys.

She greeted them, wheezing. 'Cheryl's moving up Yarmouth next week.' Deep lines ran down from the corners of her mouth. 'Long way off. I won't see Troy that much.'

'He's a real chatterbox these days,' said Eve to her as they continued up the stairs. 'I'll miss him too.'

On the top landing Knox hugged her. 'Everyone except us is moving away from this house. Even the Tomblings are going to their daughter's. Rats leaving the sinking ship do you think?'

'No. It's fate. Strand House is going from strength to strength. You are going to own it all. The name will have to be changed to Knox Palace.'

'You bet. Now I must get back to my blasted work.' He kissed her and disappeared into his flat.

Eve had plenty to do. Not only was she coordinating the builders, plumbers and electricians working on various parts of the house, but she was also painting ceilings and walls herself. Being a perfectionist, she spent hours repairing ceiling mouldings and fiddling with small brushes to get the effect she wanted. She'd even hired a machine to sand the floors.

There was no time for her own canvases. She had written a letter resigning from her job at the city college and looked forward to giving up teaching. There were so many plans in her head for the house, she found herself excited. Knox gave her a free hand, but with limits as to expense, and for the first time in her life she could decorate to suit her own taste.

She'd stopped writing the Jez emails, but still often thought of her. Being able to talk to Knox about her helped. And all the time she was so busy.

She glanced out of the window. With the Tomblings leaving, she would be responsible for the garden too. All her favourite trees, shrubs and flowers would soon be growing there.

Feeling her skin glow and prickle with joy, she couldn't stop smiling. Her happiness came from her feelings for Knox. She knew she was in love with him. With the slant of his jaw, the muscle power of his body, his authoritarian approach. The way he knew what he wanted. She loved everything about him. All her perceptions were heightened and she felt alive. She was at the centre of his universe and he was at the centre of hers. For the first time in her life, she felt powerful, even immortal.

On one of her city days, she went shopping in her lunch hour and ran into Simon at the bank.

'Hi,' he called to her. 'You look amazingly well. No need to ask how you're doing.'

'Thanks. You look great yourself. How's Florence?'

'Wonderful. I've met a beautiful Pre-Raphaelite red-haired girl. I can't wait to get back to her,' he tucked his wallet in his jacket pocket. 'I'm just home for the weekend.'

'How's your Aunt Venetia?' I shouldn't have asked that, thought Eve.

'Well, as always. Despite the fact that she's divorcing her husband. Though really, she doesn't approve of divorce. Says she's driven to it because he's a waster who's let her down. But I found him a laugh. And clever. Anyway, she's become more friendly with a neighbour she's known for years. A widower. The owner of North Runton Manor. So I imagine she'll be getting married again eventually. He's a bit more staid and will suit her better. They'll be pillars of respectability together in North Norfolk.'

'That's good news then.' She was unaccountably pleased. 'Must be off. Good luck with your studies.'

She finished her shopping and went back to college singing loudly, not caring who heard.

It was the anniversary of her arrival at Strand House and she had invited Hester to join her and Knox for supper.

On her way home she picked up the fresh sea bass she'd ordered from Shipden's best fishmonger. It was chosen to please Knox.

As soon as she arrived in her flat, she cooked, preparing Chinese-style green vegetables and rice, then chopping up root ginger and onions to put in the fish before steaming it whole in dry white wine. Collecting spring onions and soy sauce, she set the table. She'd made fresh pineapple sorbet with lemons and egg whites the night before. This is the food of love, she thought.

The last of the evening sun streamed through the window and made the table glow as the three of them sat eating and talking. As darkness fell, Eve lit candles and brought in Brie and Camembert cheeses and coffee.

'I heard today that Choker and Venetia are getting divorced,' she said.

'Yes. About time.' Hester stared at the candlelight. 'Choker's had enough of her. Far too conventional and stultifyingly boring for him. Can't imagine why he stayed with her so long. He's in north London now. Fixing up a place we're buying together. My sons aren't ecstatic about the arrangement, to be honest.' She blew smoke into her coffee. 'But I'm looking forward to living with him at last. He's good company and we've known each other for ever.'

Eve turned away to hide her shock.

'And there's your book launch coming up this year. He can support you with all that,' said Knox, putting an arm round Hester's shoulder.

'That's right. I'm getting excited already about it. Lots of my old friends have been ringing up. I'll be in the thick of things again. Makes me feel younger.' She laughed. 'Don't you ever miss London, Eve?'

'No. I have everything I want here in Shipden.' Eve smiled at Knox. But all the same she felt a strange loss.

April

It was the night of Hester's going-away party. She'd hired the small ballroom in a cliff top hotel, plus a four-piece band that specialised in 1960s hits, then she'd invited everyone she knew. A huge number.

Standing very upright in the doorway to greet her guests, wearing a silky, black, low-cut dress and high heels, Hester looked like a celebrity. Loudly, amusingly, she introduced people, showed them where to sit and organised their drinks.

The band members were strumming and tuning on a dais surrounded by dusty potted palms at the end of the room. Red velvet window curtains were closed against the cold darkness, stunted trees and crashing waves outside. Within all was warm and fragrant, the shabbiness of worn plush furniture, chipped stucco and tarnished mirror-gilding hidden under the dim red, pink and gold lighting.

Eve was enjoying herself immensely. She and Knox sat at Hester's table next to an ancient Russian couple called Vladimir and Moussia who described themselves as sibling sculptors, eking out a living in a nearby barn conversion. Their shaggy hair gave them identical white lion's manes, and Vlad's walnut face was nearly obscured behind his flowing, snowy, biblical beard. They had brought a flask of their own homemade potato vodka and tossed back the little full glasses with nonchalant abandon as they exchanged jokes in loud, fractured English with Grace and Vernon. Above the table the air crackled with laughter.

Vlad turned to Eve. 'We saw you before at Hester's, a year since. You were thin, tense, miserable, I think. Now we see you, happy face. Is it because this strong young man is here?'

She blushed and Knox laughed.

'I drink to you, Eve.' Vlad bowed his head gallantly.

It was true, she felt in a heightened happiness. She was

attracted to Knox all the time and she could tell he felt the same. They could hardly stop touching and holding each other, from the first time they had slept together. Love is surrendering oneself completely, she thought, I can't help putting him first now. With difficulty she disengaged her eyes from his and looked around.

Cheryl, too, had returned from Yarmouth for the occasion, without Dave. 'He's sitting Troy,' she explained to Eve, then resumed her conversation with a young gay man called Bobbin, one of Hester's great friends, who kept Cheryl amused with tales of his life as a trainee chef.

What a huge and amazing crowd, thought Eve, looking round at the mostly unfamiliar guests. The majority of Hester's friends were creative people: novelists, painters, etchers, wood carvers, potters and poets. There were also an assortment of kitchen staff, psychiatrists, vicars, teachers, care-workers, students, window-cleaners, eccentrics and people from all walks of life who'd come from the further reaches of north Norfolk. Some wore kaftans and drifty ethnic clothing, some young girls favoured mini-skirts, some old men had rediscovered their velvet or corduroy suits, a couple of Gothic women came in fish nets and tutus.

Knox bought a bottle of champagne for Hester who came and sat with them. She was animated and amusing, her eyes glittering behind swathes of free-falling dark hair. She looked younger and more graceful than Eve had seen her before. In the soft glow, as Hester waved her bangled arms, her diamond rings casting glistening facets of light, Eve saw that her friend must have been beautiful in her youth.

'I've had too many horses' necks tonight. Since the Navy introduced me to the medicinal benefits of brandy and dry ginger, so long ago, I've been a great fan. But I like champagne more. Thank you.' Hester put her glass down as the band struck up. 'This is my music.'

The notes of Elvis Presley's *Heartbreak Hotel* swooped

around them.

'When I was young, we danced round our handbags to this.' She pushed back her chair and danced by herself on the empty floor, her shoulders hunched, her knees together, her slim hips moving back and forth seductively. She sang the words as she moved.

The loudness of the music made conversation impossible. The hypnotic rhythm called them and people surged onto the floor to dance. Eve and Knox twirled energetically, avoiding a fair girl in a halter top who flung her arms around crazily, creating a hazard as she twisted and juddered. The blonde's back had been tattooed to create an effect of violet lace that rippled with her spine. Interlocked couples shuffled. Each person danced in the style of his or her youth, and not one appeared inhibited. The vodka put fire in the steps of the Russians, and Moussia clapped and called her brother 'Vaslav Nijinsky' as he skipped about.

Eve remembered how Choker had danced with her. His gliding style smooth and suave, unlike Knox's, which owed more to strength and athleticism than sophistication. She moved closer to Knox, pressing her body against his, wanting to feel at one with him.

Why isn't Choker here? she wondered. Then realised what it would be like. Choker sitting at the same table as Hester, Cheryl and herself. Choker looking at the three women, one after the other. Choker dancing with them one after the other. Each woman thinking her own thoughts. Each woman having her own private view and memories of the man.

What he thought no one ever knew.

Eve was thankful he wasn't there. Knox had never seen her with the poet. She didn't want to give anything away, in her eyes or body language.

She wondered what Hester knew. And what Cheryl thought. All she understood at that moment was that she loved Knox as she'd never loved Choker. And yet there was still something, which made her still think about him. A dangerous man. She was well rid of him.

Hester was having great fun. She hardly stopped dancing all night. She and Bobbin evolved a complicated jive step, with much to and fro-ing and twizzling that had her doubled up out of breath. Then she rushed off round the tables, chattering to everyone and inviting them to dance or eat.

During the band breaks when conversation was possible, Eve was talking more and more to Vlad. He'd discovered from Hester that Eve had painted the series of shellfish abstracts in the hotel dining room that he'd seen earlier and admired. After they'd discussed art works a while, he stared at her, almost rudely, then leaned across the table and spoke rapidly to Moussia in Russian. She too stared at Eve and nodded to her brother.

'You come see us, next week. Tuesday.' She said to Eve. 'I draw map,' and proceeded to don horn-rimmed spectacles and draw on her paper napkin.

Eve, intrigued, agreed to a time, thanked her and slipped the map into her pocket.

The party lasted into the small hours, until Hester was in a state of collapse and had to be put to bed by Grace and Vernon, the most sober guests.

The next morning being Sunday there was no need to get up early, but when Eve woke with the birds she was nauseous; she climbed out of bed, careful not to wake Knox.

She vomited in the bathroom and felt better. I'm not used to being on the razzle, she thought ruefully and went in the kitchen to make a mug of tea.

The sun cast spangles on the sea and the day looked so inviting she dressed and went to walk on the beach.

There was not a soul around, but plenty of birdsong on the cliffs, and down below gulls sat silently on the rippling waves.

In the peace, she found herself thinking first of Jez, then her mother. If only they could be with me now and share in my happiness, she wished. I was so close to Jez and I'm sure that if my mother had lived longer, I would have been closer to her, too. I never really understood my mother, what made her happy or sad. She told me a lot of strange things. Things I learned later weren't true. But she just wanted to protect me, I suppose. She'd be about Hester's age if she were alive. But not like Hester. She never had that confidence. No family or money behind her. Everything she achieved, she did by herself, but she was unsure of which way to go. Eve remembered how she'd looked after her fragile mother as though she were her child instead of the other way about.

She sighed and walked on for a mile, then back.

On her return, Knox was just stirring. She kissed him. 'Coffee?'

'Mm. Eggs and bacon, too.'

'If you insist. You have a strong constitution.' As she took off her jacket the nauseous feeling returned. 'I've been for a walk. When I came in just now, I thought the outside of the house was looking grey and shabby with bits of rendering falling off all over the place. Can we paint it all white? Walls and windows?'

'You bet. It's almost ours now. Shall we change the name?'

'We could, because it's a new start.' She pondered. 'You know the castle keep in the city? When the Normans built it, in the twelfth century I think, the stone facing from Caen was pale, so they called it Blanchfleur.'

'White Flower. I like it. White's the sign of purity and peace. Appropriate. You're the lady of my castle. We'll give it the old name Blanchfleur in your honour.'

'Thank you.'

On Tuesday Knox went to work in the University library.

Before he left Eve reminded him it was her day to visit the Russians. He lowered his bicycle handlebars and saddle, as her legs were so much shorter than his.

The wind blew briskly as she cycled along the empty country lanes on his bike. Hazel catkins swung and new green leaves sprouted on the thin twigs and branches of trees that leaned away from the sea. Lambs sprang about, making surprised squeaks and bleats, and running to their loud mothers for reassurance. Pigs rooted about in the dark earth, grunting their satisfaction. Ragged clouds sailed above. The air smelled sweet and clear.

After consulting her map a few times, Eve found the great barn, hidden and solitary in a field, behind trees down a cart track. Arriving, breathless, she leaned the bike against the old flint wall and pulled off her backpack.

Moussia emerged, kissed her on both cold cheeks and led her inside by the hand.

Half of the barn had been made into a studio with windows down one side. A wood-burning stove threw out heat. Great clay models stood on the concrete floor, figures of giant men being built up. There was a rectilinear lump of stone with outlines, and someone had partly blocked out an abstract form with a stonemason's hammer. Punches, mallets and chisels lay about among the chips of stone. Armatures, metal skeletons, stooped in threatening postures. Small wax effigies and a bronze jaguar stood on shelves at one end. At the other end stacks of tiles leaned on tables, some tiles painted with brilliant designs and fired. Some items were shrouded in canvas. A kiln stood at the back. Everything was covered in grey dust.

'Vlad is carver. I, modeller,' Moussia explained. 'Come this way.' She opened a heavy oak door in the studio wall.

The other half of the barn made up the living quarters. Worn hand-woven rugs covered a tiled floor. There were sagging sofas and Indian carved cupboards and tables, with elaborate embroidered hangings and Russian icons and paintings on the white rough-plastered or flint walls. Bookcases held collections of stones and animal skulls on top. An untidy kitchen with bunches of herbs hanging from the ceiling, and next to it, a closed door, were, visible at the back, a wooden staircase led up to an open gallery bedroom under the roof. Everything was dusty and in disorder. Eve loved it.

'This is charming,' she said. 'I envy you your home.'

'Is not always so easy,' said Vlad, waving a hand at the small, unheated kitchen. 'Have drink?'

A jug of black liquid heavy with sediment sat on the pot-bellied stove. Together they sent out an agreeable and pungent odour of burning fruit wood and hot coffee.

Moussia brought six tiny, gold, porcelain cups and the three of them drank the strong sweet coffee with a colourless and fiery spirit she described as 'plums'.

'Wonderful,' said Eve, feeling light-headed. 'Best coffee and plums I've had.' She emptied her backpack and gave the old lady a load of assorted literary and art magazines that had originally been passed on by Hester, and a cinnamon cake she'd baked the day before.

'Now we show you things,' said Vlad after half an hour, and creaked to his feet, putting down his pipe.

Both he and his sister wore venerable tweed garments that appeared home-made, and carpet slippers of genuine old carpet.

Eve was concerned. 'How do you manage here, so far from the nearest village?'

But it seemed that the owner of the local shop was a friend who delivered nearly all they needed, and behind the barn was a rather weed-filled vegetable garden and a few fruit trees. Beyond the washing, which fluttered madly on the line at the back, stood a well and an outhouse containing sacks of potatoes and carrots.

Eve, fascinated by the paintings and icons on the walls,

studied them intently. The light, pouring through the wall of glass, shone clearly on the variety of art works. She especially liked a small oil painting of tulips in jewel colours against a black background. It was signed A.T. Next to it hung a framed pencil drawing with the same initials, dated 1961, to which she found herself attracted. The subject was a nude lying on a bed, a young girl supporting her head on one delicate hand. She looked directly into the eyes of the artist, unsmiling, rather like Manet's *Olympia*, and round her slight neck was tied a lace of dark ribbon.

Eve started at the instant recognition.

'You like that?' asked Vlad.

'Very much,' said Eve. 'Who was the model, do you know?'

He shrugged. 'There were many different ones.'

'Do you have any more work by the same artist?'

'No, sadly. That's Alex Temple. He was friend of us. Died about 1980.'

'I've not heard of him.'

'Was not well known.' He picked up his pipe and started to light it again. 'We lived in Paris many years. Our parents white Russians. Then we moved to London. Met Alex there in sixties. We knew his woman, Katya—also Russian—a long time.'

'That drawing. Is it of Katya?'

Moussia came up beside them and laughed. She spoke in Russian to her brother, then turned to Eve. 'No. Katya was older, black hair, not fair. Very jealous. Didn't like his pictures of other women.'

Eve's heart was beating an irregular metre. She remembered well how her mother used to wear a black ribbon round her neck. It wasn't a fashionable thing at the time, but her mother never cared about what other people did, only what suited her. 'Do you have a photo of Alex Temple?'

Vlad rooted round in a woodwormed desk and found a large coloured photograph of the artist standing with two handsome black-haired women on a city pavement. Eve recognised the much younger Moussia at once. The other woman presumably was Katya. She turned her attention to the man. He appeared about forty, with strong features, receding hair, a humorous expression and distinctive, deep-set, light duck-egg blue eyes. She didn't recall ever seeing him before.

'Was always laughing, Alex,' said Vlad, scrutinising her in the bright light. 'You have same colour eyes. Unusual.' He puffed at his pipe.

Eve thought, yes. And my front teeth overlap slightly just like his. 'What did he die of?'

'He travelled to Africa. Had tropical fever there.'

Eve felt strange, a little faint. 'I must go, but thank you so much for your kindness. May I come and see you another time?'

'Of course.'

In the fresh air she felt better. She cycled slowly home, thinking about her mother. As she pedalled, she ordered her thoughts. My mother always said she didn't know my father, so there was no use in searching for him. Because she always drank so much and took any drugs going, and she was a party girl, she said. Anyway, it was the sixties and seventies and she enjoyed herself like crazy and those dull farts who remembered what they did in those decades must have had a bloody boring time. That's what she said. She didn't have the faintest idea who my father was because she'd had a marvellous time and slept with hordes of men, had the pick of the best-looking wealthy men in London.

I should think of her as a *femme du monde,* a loving woman who had the capacity to run relationships concurrently. That's what I should think.

But even that may not have been true. Maybe she fell in

love with one of the artists who paid her to pose for him. Maybe he felt something special for her. Perhaps they had a loving and exclusive affair.

And I'm here, now, cycling along this pot-holed lane with the sun high, shining on me, and I'm interested in art, always have been since I could first hold a crayon in my fingers. And she, my mother, didn't like to draw or paint and never looked at art works, just her reflection in the mirror. Why did I become a painter? It wasn't instilled into me that I had to do that. I just wanted to—and perhaps that was because I inherited those genes.

I could find out more about my past. For the first time I really want to know more.

That drawing is of my mother. I'm sure. The shock of recognition made my heart judder. The man who drew her so sympathetically must have felt something for her. I owe it to myself to learn more.

Slowly she cycled home, in and out of the shadows.

Hi Hester,

You asked me to email you, so here I am. How are things with you? Are you settling in? Good neighbours? Strand House is so different now with everyone gone except Knox and me. Not quiet. The builders and workmen see to that. But everything is so changed. I miss you and your wise, white witch words. Knox is so busy with his course. Virtually no holidays during the year and he always has so much to do. He talks to me about presentations of solutions he has to do, about modules concerning human resources, marketing, finance and statistics. But it all means so little to me that I'm afraid I'm no help at all. However, I am organising the house changes for him. You must come back and stay with us sometime and see what we're doing. I miss our long talks. I remember Grace saying once, 'Everyone tells everything to Hester. She's so patient and never interrupts.' It's true. You were everyone's confidante here. I've become friendly with Vlad and

Moussia Miansarow. They have warm hearts and mine is unfreezing all the time. It's odd, I like writing emails because I can be free. As a rather inhibited person, I find face-to-face communication difficult. But I enjoy writing and I can be 'talkative' this way. Have you heard of an artist called Alex Temple? Dead now, but he was a friend of the Miansarows when they lived in London. I just wondered if you'd come across him there. I like his work.

Love to you both, Eve.

My dear Eve,

It's splendid to have news of you. I miss you, too, and the sea and the fresh air of north Norfolk. Poor Pluto, my dearest dark prince, also misses those long walks on the beach and marshes. Walks in these city parks aren't nearly so exciting. But he's continually making new friends among the rough sleepers. Our place is almost organised already. I hate living in a mess. We have only one large bedroom, so visitors will have to use the pull-out sofa bed in our living room (great balcony and window boxes there). We've had to divide the dining room to make two studies as Choker and I need our own space. Mine is cool and pale, full of books, photos of Hugo and your wonderful dog Conversazione. His, naturally, is purple and mirrored, full of books and his special dragon 'muse' desk. Not that he spends much time in his study. He walks a lot, at night, and writes in his notebook as he goes. At least he's back to writing. He did a reading at The Voice Box on the South Bank last Saturday evening. It went well, warm audience, except afterwards some stupid bitch asked me if I was his mother. Can you imagine? I mopped the floor with her. She'll think before she opens her mouth again. He has readings booked all over the country in the next few months, to promote his latest collection. He also has some teaching set up and manuscript assessment, as well as his reviewing. So he'll be busy. My publisher, Jen, is a sweetie. Flaxen haystack hair and sympathetic eyes. We go out to lunch all the time. Choker and I eat out, too, neither of us can be bothered

to cook. As you know I lived on boiled eggs and gin in Shipden.
Restaurants and bistros are excellent. Transport's interesting. As
always, I refuse to go on the back of Choker's repellent motorbike,
and he can't abide the Morris Traveller. We intend to flog both
and invest in a nippy city car. Black, to please you-know-who. He
quite fancies an old taxi cab. We've met some Hampstead folk,
evil some of them, but that's better than being boring. Not many
saints around. I did meet Alex Temple once, long ago. Bit of a
ladies' man, good fun. Had some Russian harridan with him,
watching him like a vulture, a sort of Baba Yaga. If I ever come
across any of his paintings, I'll let you know.
Love to you and Knox.
Hester. (Choker sends a big kiss).

Eve sat on the beach at the water's edge, exhausted at the end
of a day spent in the company of a hired sanding machine.
Her limbs ached and her head felt full of dust.

The air swirled, cool and misty, around her and the noise
of the breakers curiously deadened.

Thinking of the past, she had a picture in her mind's eye
of black tunnel walls rushing past. She recalled standing on a
tube train seat, staring out of the window glass. She must, she
thought, have been small, as her mother, a giant, sat beside
her. The hypnotic rat-a-tat rattle of the train wheels made
her sleepy and the journey lasted a long time.

At all the stations she watched the crowd of passengers
surge off and on the train, and push along the platform. At
one stop a little boy wearing round spectacles blew chewing
gum bubbles at her from the station on the other side of the
glass. She was watching him when, to her horror, she saw her
own mother walking past the window. Her mother grinned
and as the doors slammed, she waved goodbye. As the train
moved off, Eve turned to find the seat beside her empty. The
carriage sped away, faster and faster.

The panic and desolation were vivid. And familiar. Was

this just a recurring dream, or had the incident happened when she was an infant? Eve shut her eyes in an attempt to dispel the awful picture.

When she opened her eyes, she was surrounded by white. A sea fog was rolling in. The waves whispered blindly. The larks had stopped singing. The blue sky had dissolved.

She struggled to her feet and hesitantly stepped back over the sand, making her way with difficulty back to the safety of the concrete promenade.

May

The early evening scent of lilac hung over the park. Heavy mauve and white blossoms drooped among pale green leaves where Eve breathed in the heady fragrance. High above, swifts shrieked and swooped in the warm air. Below, bumblebees patrolled the clusters of plush wallflowers under clouds of rusty pink tamarisk.

She walked slowly barefooted under the flowering chestnut trees, thinking how glad she was that she'd reached her last term of teaching. There were only a few more sessions at the college before the students' exams. Her feet ached, she felt so tired, and there was still so much to do at the house. Her bags of papers, books and shoes dragged on her arms.

Ahead of her a small purple child emerged from a clump of lilac bushes. He wore a huge, horned space-alien mask. 'Stop!' He accosted her, pointing a plastic weapon at her head.

Patiently she put down her bags and held up her hands in surrender.

He laughed. 'It's me. Me.'

'Who's me? I don't know anyone called me.'

'Yes. You silly, you.' He threw his gun down and pulled his mask off.

'Troy! Now I recognise you. With your proper face. What a good surprise. What are you doing here?'

His round face was shiny red and his lurid t-shirt and shorts smeared with dirt.

'Me playin here. Fightin baddies.'

'Where's Cheryl?'

He shrugged. 'Me thirsty.'

'Have you been here a long time?'

'Yus.' He scowled. Tear stains streaked his cheeks.

She looked round the park. There was no one.

'I wonder where she's gone.'

He stuck out his bottom lip.

'You can come home with me and have a drink.'

He picked up his mask and weapon. 'Good.' He pointed at a bush. 'Me peed there.' Then he turned round and indicated a far shed. 'And me peed behind there.'

Without commenting she took his hot hand in hers and they set off. As they approached the park gates, Cheryl crossed the road unsteadily towards them on high-heeled mules. Her complexion looked pasty and blemished, her normally bright eyes dull and unfocused, half hidden behind tangles of lustreless copper hair. She'd lost weight and her long legs under a short denim skirt were bony and frail.

'Hi, Eve,' she said. One of her false eyelashes had come unstuck and drooped teasingly from one eye.

'Troy was on his own in the park.' Eve's tone was cold.

'Yes. We come from the station and his legs was worn out. Didn't have the buggy. So he stayed here for a rest.' She didn't look at him. 'Wasn't goin to drag him all that way up my Mum's, was I? Anyway, she int in. Waste of time. He likes playin in parks. Don't you?' She looked fiercely at her son.

He fiddled with his mask. 'Me hungry.'

'How long has he been there?'

'I dunno. Not long. Couple hours tops.'

'But he's only two, for heaven's sake.' Eve tried to keep her voice calm.

'Two and a half!' bawled Troy.

'Shut up, you,' said Cheryl. She turned to Eve. 'It's safe. There int no paedo-thingies round here.'

'How do you know? Or he could have had an accident, or wandered off into the traffic. I just can't believe you left him on his own.'

'You better believe it. He can look after himself. He's not

one of those snotty little spoilt posh kids. He does as he's told. He's got sense.'

More than you have, thought Eve.

But Cheryl's trembling turned to shaking. 'It's none of your bloody business. You int got no kids. Don't know what it's like, having one hang onto your skirt and whinin all day and every day. Does my head in.' She shouted right in Eve's face. 'You take the little bugger. You look after him. Then you'll see what it's like.' And she wheeled around and rushed off zigzagging round the corner.

Troy's face crumpled. 'Cherl!' he called, but still gripped Eve's hand and made no attempt to follow his mother.

Eve wiped the spit from her face with the back of her hand and took a deep breath. 'She's not very well.' She smiled down at the little boy. 'So we'll leave her to get better. And you and I can go to my flat and have some scrambled egg on toast. I might even have some ice cream there. You remember my flat, you've been there lots of times. But not recently.'

His expression was more hopeful. 'Me thirsty.'

'I have plenty of milk, too.' She bent and pushed her painful feet into her shoes. 'Let's go.' She felt a terrible pity for him, remembering how, as a small child, the all-consuming love for one's mother could be tested to breaking point.

Later that night, when he slept, curled under a quilt on her living room sofa, she watched him in the glow of a nightlight. His hair stuck up in tufts, his thumb in his mouth, and his expression calm.

She returned to the kitchen, picked up the newspaper and read that yet another child had vanished. That familiar, old heartache. More parents would be feeling that intense, gut-wrenching panic as horrific possibilities occurred to them: an accident, an abduction, a murder. People would be searching night and day, suffering the agony of not knowing what had happened.

Eve thought first of infant Jez and how she'd worried about her, then of Troy left to fend for himself. Cheryl was vulnerable and in no state to care for her son. Eve wondered what she could be doing, whether she was safe. She made up her mind to ring the social services in the morning, to tell them what she knew and to make her care of Troy official.

She phoned Cheryl's mother a few times during the evening, but no one responded and there was no answering service. Her stomach was full of acid so she ate liquorice sweets, her usual comfort.

Knox was working on an assignment in his old flat. He and Eve planned to bring his single bed into her living room the next day, so Troy could be more comfortable.

She wanted the boy as near as possible to her bedroom so that she and Knox could hear him if he woke at night.

Before the child fell asleep, he seemed happy enough, accepting everything she suggested without question, enjoying his supper, games and splashy bath. He remembered the house well, and her flat. To her surprise he never mentioned his mother. But when he lay down, he asked, 'Where's bear?'

'He's not here, I'm afraid, but you can have my pig for company.'

She fetched a small, orange velvet, homemade pig Knox had found on a charity stall and given her. It was soft and round with a curly wool tail and a disproportionately large snout. It gave a guttural honk when squeezed, like their neighbour summoning his cat. 'This pig's called Mr Godsmark.'

'Like the next-door man.'

'Yes. Fancy you remembering his name.'

Troy made Mr Godsmark honk a few times, then tucked him under his chin.

She went back to the kitchen and stared out of the window.

Night smothered the day relentlessly. The sky darkened. Leaden fingers of cloud stretched from the horizon and overpowered the last shreds of twilight.

A nightingale croaked an alarm call from hawthorn bushes.

She watched the sea blacken, the lights in the Godsmark house turn off below.

Eventually Knox joined her. 'I can't do any more tonight. Let's go to bed.' He put his coffee mug in the sink. 'Troy's fast asleep.'

'I want to look after that child.'

'I know you do.'

'I mean, permanently. If we're allowed.'

'I understand.' He put his arms round her. 'That's fine by me. I like him, too. I always liked him. Cheryl's not a fit mother. Troy won't come between us. We'll still have time together. But it's still a big responsibility.'

'It's just that we have so much. This huge house. With all these empty rooms. I want to fill them with unwanted children.' Tears came into her eyes.

He stared down at her. 'Eve, I have something to ask you. I know we've never discussed it, but my divorce is through. I've just got my decree absolute. I'm a free man again. Would you consider marrying me as soon as possible?' As an afterthought he went down on one knee and leaned his head against her stomach.

She thought he might be afraid to look her in the eye, so quickly replied, 'Yes,' and stroked his hair. 'Thank you for asking.'

'My pleasure. I love you.' His voice was muffled. 'We could be married in that flint Register Office on the cliff. Let's declare our intention tomorrow. It takes a few days.'

The Georgian building was surrounded by rose gardens. 'I can't think of anywhere I'd rather be married in. As it happens, I love you, too.'

'Let's do it then. I went in to talk to them ages ago.'

'Before you asked me? You're very sure of yourself. What if I'd said no.'

'I never allow myself to have negative thoughts. I'm sure of you. As soon as I saw you holding my measuring tape, I knew I'd found my second Mrs Smith. I'm just sorry it's taken me so long to get around to asking.'

'I've something to tell you.' Her heart was pounding.

'I thought you might.' He looked straight at her and smiled.

'I'm pregnant.'

'I guessed already.' He kissed her. 'And I couldn't be happier. I'll look after you and the baby.' He grinned. 'We'll be brilliant parents. When's it due?'

'Around November, I think. You know what a scatterbrain I am.' She was nervous. I'm too old for this lark, she thought.

As if he knew what was going through her mind, he said, 'It'll be like falling off a log. You've done it before.'

'Over two decades ago. Not exactly yesterday.' She touched his neck. 'I find you irresistible.'

'Lucky for me.' He held her closely. 'You must see the doctor tomorrow.'

She detached herself and went to the bathroom. Her face in the mirror was pink and glowing, her eyes gleaming with tears. She didn't remember being so excited before, or so apprehensive. There was a new, tiny being inside her, a new personality, a new life like no other. She was aware she'd become sensitive to criticism, worried over trifles, laughed at nothing and wept at much. Aware that between herself and the creature inside, there was the beginning of a new relationship. Conscious that for some weeks she'd been on a journey of surprises, one day craving cockles and mussels, another feeling a violent aversion to the smell of meat in a butcher's shop. She felt as though she was a different person.

But there is a different person, she thought, the one inside. This tiny creature is directing me. Everything is altered for the better. When I was expecting Jez, I was ill and afraid. On my own. It's not like that now. It's my second chance. I shall be with Knox for ever and we will care for each other. We'll be a real family.

The week was wet. Every day they woke to rain pattering on the windows.

Eve met various people from social services. It was agreed she and Knox could continue to look after Troy meantime, as the boy didn't want to leave them. Police checks had to be made on both of them. Cheryl's mother had been discovered in a hospital on the other side of the country, and Cheryl herself had disappeared again. She'd apparently moved out of Dave's flat in Yarmouth some weeks ago, and he had no knowledge of her since then. He'd denied fathering Troy and refused to accept any responsibility for the child.

Cheryl was well known to the social services. She had in the past been offered parenting classes she'd refused, and had the option of her son being taken into care.

The boy trotted round the empty rooms in Blanchfleur, making friends with the middle-aged builder who was still taking down dividing partitions.

'Look, Tom. My room.' In his old bedroom he pointed out vomit stains on the wall. 'Me sick there.'

'Oh, boy. That's champion. So you slept here before.'

'Yes.'

'And now you're upstairs.'

'Me big now.'

'So you are. You'll soon be up to the top of the door.' He picked up a stack of wood.

'Come on, Troy. The rain's stopped. Let's go and get you some new clothes. First, we can go down and watch the crab boats come in,' said Eve, holding her hand to him.

'There aren't many of the old crabbers left now,' said Tom. 'Those double-ended ones have been used since the 1800s, but they can't be launched and landed single-handed. Because fishing goes on all year now people want more speed and room.' He stretched. 'My brother's a fisherman and wants a boat he can handle himself, and use for netting and lining for white fish and skate, as well as crabbing.'

'Yes, I'd noticed the new ones,' said Eve.

She and Troy wandered down to the sea, feeling the damp wind in their faces. Sand martins were feeding at the cliff edge and swallows flew over the greens. Young surfers in wetsuits bobbed on the waves below the big hotel. Square-backed skiffs and catamarans were pulled up on the wet beach alongside the old crabbers, which mirrored the shape of Viking long ships.

A new fibreglass craft with a wheelhouse wind shelter on the front came round the pier and up to the edge of the sand and the fisherman waded out of the water and up the beach to drive the tractor down and hoist the skiff onto its carriage.

'I suppose the new boats can go further. And they're probably safer,' said Eve.

'That white one is best.' Troy waved to the fisherman. 'Me want to go on that one.'

'Sorry, it's not allowed. But we can go on a canoe on the pond. Would you like that?'

They slowly walked up the slope. As she glanced sideways at the sea, Eve fancied she saw rows of old-fashioned bathing huts. She rubbed her eyes and the scene was normal again. She thought of the early nineteenth century when men came to Shipden for heated sea baths and took sea water in the hope of curing their sexually transmitted diseases. She wondered who had told her that. Hester, of course, fount of much odd knowledge.

Hi Hester,

It's me again with news from Shipden. I'm enjoying my freedom, only two more teaching days left now, then I just have exam marking and reference writing and I'll be finished. Just as well, as it happens, because I'm looking after Troy full-time. On my two days in the city, Knox can take care of him. Cheryl's in a bad way now. She's done another of her disappearing tricks, as has her mother. I really enjoy having a child around. It reminds me of bringing up Jez when she was a tiny girl. He's a funny little chap, talks much more now. At first he was a bit weepy and demanding and had bad dreams. He said No to everything, but now he's learned to fall in with all my suggestions so we don't have confrontations. Small children are easily distracted. No doubt my expectations of him are not the same as Cheryl's, but he's insecure and needy. I expect I'm overprotective. Knox thinks I'm a bit soft on him. I've invited the Miansarows for Sunday lunch. Knox will drive them over and back. They're both a bit fragile-seeming at the moment, arthritic and using sticks. Yet remember how they danced at your party?

You'll never guess what's happening next. Or perhaps you will. Knox and I have decided to get married. Second time round for both of us. What do people call it, the triumph of hope over experience? Something like that. Anyway, we're both very happy. We're old enough to know what we want. The only fly in the ointment concerns his future job. He's about to get his business degree, all being well, but there's no suitable employment for him round here, no big companies at all. So he'll have to work in London. Commuting every day would be exhausting, so he'll probably only be back at weekends. Having found what he describes as the perfect place to live, he doesn't want to move. We're almost finished re-jigging the house, and the rooms we've decorated look good. I'm sick of the smell of emulsion and gloss paint, and of doing the garden. I'd never appreciated how much the Tomblings did out there in the flowerbeds. We've only had a post card from them since they moved. They sound very pleased with life. Hope you are. With love, Eve.

My dear Eve and Knox,
A thousand congratulations! How clever of you to decide to get married. You'll be the perfect couple and the Lord and Lady of Shipden. Let me know when the big day is to be, won't you? By chance I've found you the ideal wedding present and I'll bring it up in person before long. Glad to hear about Troy, too. Poor little sod always needed someone sensible to mother him. Sorry about Cheryl. She's her own worst enemy. Hope she grows up soon. What happens when she wants him back? If she does. Have to say I've matured in the last few weeks. What a learning curve! Choker and I have had the parting of the ways. Living together just didn't work out, so he's moved away. In fact, I don't know where he is. Luckily, I can afford to stay here without his contribution. I just didn't have the stamina for his life style. A bit too reminiscent of my life with Hugo, to be honest, and I've decided I need peace and quiet and a decent night's sleep now and then. I've loads of friends here, so I'm not lonely at all. And my sons have taken to calling on me again. They never approved of Choker. So I'm back in favour with my family. Dear Pluto is my stalwart companion. We're off for a walk on the Heath. It's always good to have news of you. I'll come and see you soon. Much love, Hester.

June

Heat vibrated from the concrete platform at Shipden station. Knox, Eve and Troy retreated to the three-sided brick shelter to escape the disturbing rays of the sun. Apart from them the place was deserted. There was no ticket office or, indeed, ticket collector. A few tubs of multicoloured geraniums and petunias wilted by a litterbin and a wooden seat. Above, near the horizon, three white puffs of cloud were immobile in the blue, as though stuck to the sky.

Troy sucked the last drops of water from his personal bottle through a curly straw. 'More,' he demanded.

'Please,' said Eve.

'More,' he said loudly. 'Please,' quietly.

She refilled his small bottle from a large one, then leaned back to feel the coolness of the brick wall.

'I should quite like you to pour the rest of that over my head.' Knox sat still, saving his energy.

'Have a cold shower when we get back. I'm not wasting this.'

'You're a cruel and unfeeling woman.'

'That's right.' She blew him a kiss.

'Hurry up, old train.' Troy stuck his head out impatiently. Then, 'It's coming now.'

Sure enough, the track trembled and they could all hear a rattle down the line.

A two-coach train clattered its way to the platform and stopped. The electrically operated doors slid back and a couple of girls stepped out and walked away. No one else emerged.

'Where is she?' Eve hurried the length of the train, peering in the windows.

The guard disembarked and looked around. 'You getting on?'

'No. Can you hang on a minute?' Knox joined the search.

'She's here,' Eve called. 'Just wait by the seat, Troy.'

The child stood on the platform as Knox jumped aboard with Eve.

In a corner of the carriage a woman was slumped in her seat, snoring. Her black hair tangled over her peacock blue satin blouse. Bare feet poked out below a long, shiny black skirt.

'Wake up, Hester. You're here,' called Knox, shaking her shoulder.

'Please wait. There's someone getting off,' shouted Eve to the guard who had his whistle in his mouth.

She recognised Hester's purple case on wheels and ancient hatbox, and heaved them onto the platform. Knox was having no success rousing Hester quickly enough so, finding a pair of crocodile shoes under the seat, shoved them on her feet. He hung her handbag over her arm, and, grunting with the effort, picked her up bodily and carried her off the train.

The passengers watched with interest. 'She be drunk,' growled an old man.

'About time.' The testy guard tapped his watch, blew his whistle and boarded the train. The doors slid closed and the train moved off, reverberating into the distance.

Knox deposited his load, like a sack of turnips, onto the wooden seat. The sun shone violently into Hester's eyes. 'Wha?' She moved her head.

'What's the matter wiv her?' asked Troy.

'Good question,' said Knox, showing no anxiety.

'She's sleepy,' said Eve to Troy. Then to Hester, 'You're at Shipden.'

'Already?' Hester yawned and focused on the figures round her. 'So I am.' Her speech was slurred. 'Who's this small person?'

'Me,' said Troy. 'Not small.'

Hester pulled herself to her feet and embraced them all with difficulty, before sagging back down and clutching her head. 'I need a lie-down. I met a lovely canon in the bar on the train from Liverpool Street. Delicious man. Think he had a wig. Plied me with gin all the way. It was so damned hot. Lovely tonic. The ice, you know, refreshing.' She weakly pushed her hair out of her eyes. 'Disappeared, he did. Nearly missed my connection. Some sweetie in uniform assisted me.'

'Army?' asked Knox, squinting down at her.

'Salvation, probably, or St John's Ambulance. I dunno.' She stared around her. 'God, where's my luggage?'

'Here it is,' Eve indicated behind the seat. 'Now, let's get out of the sun and back to the house.' She pulled Hester to her feet and took her arm. Knox took the other and they propelled her with difficulty along the platform and into the camper van, Troy skipping along. Then, sweating, they returned for her case and hatbox.

At the house Knox helped her in and left her on a sofa to recover.

The next morning was overcast. The doorbell rang while Hester still lay in bed. She was in a poor state, in their newly painted best spare room on the first floor. Knox had left early for the University and Troy was busy in the kitchen with his dumper trucks and toy bricks.

Eve brought the social worker into the living room. This anaemic woman had visited several times before. She wore an anonymous beige skirt and blouse. Her flesh was paper white and her grey teeth were pointed like an animal's.

'How's Troy?' She plonked herself down and dropped her bag on the floor beside her.

'He's fine. I'll call him.'

'No. Don't yet. I need to tell you something while we're alone.' She picked at her blouse buttons.

Whatever's coming? thought Eve. 'Have you found

Cheryl yet?'

'Yes. Sadly we have.' She paused and stared at Eve directly. 'Cheryl's dead.' She sniffed and her gaze wandered the room. 'She was discovered last night in a squat in Yarmouth. It's a place known to be used by addicts. She'd been taking drugs for some time. Heroin, crack and cocaine. The police had seen her around. This time she took too much heroin.'

Eve was silenced. All she could think of was Troy trundling his trucks over the kitchen floor. She could hear him there making 'brm, brm' noises. She visualised that little hollow place at the back of his neck. Shocked, she tried to make sense of the information. 'Was it deliberate, do you think?' she asked slowly.

'No. We're all sure it was an accidental overdose.'

'That's tragic. I can hardly believe it of her. She always seemed full of life. But it's true the last time I saw her she was in a bad way. Poor Cheryl. What a sad end.' Confused thoughts whirled in Eve's brain. 'She was such an attractive girl.' She remembered the clouds of copper coloured hair falling round her face. 'Does her mother know?'

'Not yet. She's in no condition to take it in. She's just had a major operation.'

'The whole thing's terrible.' Eve felt glad that she had Hester to support her.

The young woman stood. 'I'm afraid I have to go now. I have so much to do. So many urgent cases. I'll just tell the little boy about his mother. Not that he's old enough to understand, poor child. And will you carry on looking after him until we find a settled foster home?'

Eve was alarmed. 'Of course. But what do you mean about fostering? I want to care for him permanently once all the checks are done. We want to adopt him.'

'No doubt, in time. There's a lot to think about.' She

fussed about opening and shutting her bag. 'Though actually, local placements are wanted. At the moment we're sending children to live with foster carers in other counties. It's not good for their family and friends to have to go so far to visit. There aren't enough foster parents in this area.' She collected her bag and went into the kitchen to speak to Troy.

A minute later she came back. 'I must go, my boss is waiting in the car. I'll call again soon.'

Not tomorrow, I'm getting married, thought Eve. She went to pick up the puzzled child and carried him in her arms. She held the front door open as the social worker went out and climbed into the passenger seat of a dusty car.

The driver craned her neck to get a good view of Eve.

And Eve was therefore able to see clearly that the senior social worker was none other than the woman who looked like the pangolin, the one who had visited the house months previously. Her long nose twitched as she stared inquisitively then put the car in gear.

How horrible everything is, Eve thought, going back inside. Cheryl wasn't my favourite person, but I didn't want her to die, even if it means I can keep Troy forever. However did she get into such a mess? We could have helped. Now no one can. And how can I make it up to Troy now Cheryl's gone? I'll do my best to be a mother to him.

'What's going on?' Hester, fully recovered, came prancing downstairs. She wore a crisp white robe and her eyes shone, their whites like hard-boiled eggs.

'Thank God you're here. I really need your help. Something awful's happened.'

The day passed in a blur. Eve told Troy his mother had gone to heaven to live with Jesus. He said nothing, stared at the kitchen tiles.

'We'll get a lovely big photo of Cheryl and put it by your bed.'

'Did she take me bear with her?'

'I don't know. We'll go to the shops today and buy another one, just the same, I promise.'

'Can me stay here?' His eyes were big and round.

'Of course.' She hugged him.

'Can me see my Nan?'

'Yes. We'll go and see her soon. Poor Nan is ill in hospital now. But as soon as she's a bit better, I promise we'll visit. She'll be missing you.'

'Is Cherl wiv Nan?'

Eve sighed. 'No. Cheryl's in heaven. We won't be able to see your Mummy any more. But we'll see Nan.'

He looked puzzled. 'You, pieface!'

'You, sweetheart.' She kissed him and he ran off to find his toy cars.

The next day the register office was fragrant with great vases of roses. The scent followed them out to the garden where Knox and Eve drank champagne as husband and wife.

'These roses out here. Magnificent!' said Moussia, lowering her wrinkled face into red, velvety blooms.

'Watch out. Bee up your nose,' said Troy. He ran round the lawn, buzzing, his arms out, his new bear strapped to his back.

'Congratulations,' called Vlad, raising his glass to Knox. 'You are one fortunate man.'

'I know.' Knox smiled at Eve.

She felt as though she'd swallowed the sun and it glowed out of her, through her face and arms and fingers. Her sleeveless cream muslin dress swirled round her, patterned with gold embroidery at her ankles. She'd piled her long hair on top of her head and pinned it with pale silk flowers so fair tendrils fell over her eyes in wisps. She was conscious of Knox beside her all the time in his new dark suit. A strong man, she thought, feeling safe.

He set up his camera under the trees and arranged the small wedding group.

'Ready. Smile. Now.' Then he dashed back to be included in the delayed action shot.

Standing in the sunshine, for the first time she felt a fluttering, rippling in her abdomen, behind the bouquet of cream and peach roses picked from their garden. Aware of the secret movement, she thought she had never known such happiness.

After many photographs, and after Troy had tipped his boxes of confetti over them, they walked back to the house.

'Bravo, Mrs Smith. You look radiant,' called Hester, exhaling. She had chosen a dark metallic robe and an odd hat with two net horns, which made her look like a stag beetle. In her dark glasses the effect was sinister.

'Radiant youssself,' said Troy kindly, holding her hand to cross the road.

Moussia wore an ethnic purple and scarlet outfit of full skirt and waistcoat, which added to the carnival atmosphere. Vlad in his ancient white linen suit and dignified Panama hat walked with the aid of a silver-topped cane. He led the way into the house.

'You must carry the bride,' he commanded Knox.

'I hadn't forgotten.' Knox swept Eve off her feet, whirled her round, and danced through the hall. 'Light as a moth.' He set her on her feet and hugged her.

They sat at the table decorated with blossoms and candles and ate lobster salad and cold beef with home grown vine tomatoes and new potatoes from the Miansarow garden.

Eve had earlier iced the wedding cake and invited Troy to decorate it with the new plastic animals Hester had given him. He chose carefully.

'In the middle here. These two big horses.'

'They stand for Mr and Mrs Smith,' said Knox.

'So this pair of sheep is the Miansarows.' Vlad laughed.

'And I'm the spotty pig I suppose,' said Hester. 'With the disproportionately large backside.'

'Me the sheepdog.' Troy grinned.

The six animals stood serenely on the snowy icing, facing inwards, nose to nose.

'They kissing,' said Troy.

'Most suitable for a marriage,' said Knox. 'You chose well. Now help us cut the cake.'

When the meal was long over, they still sat at the table drinking brandy and coffee, while Troy played with his toy lorry on the carpet, loading it with animals and transporting them to the imaginary farm in the fireplace.

'Lord, I forgot about your wedding present.' Hester bustled upstairs and returned with a flat, square package tied up with string.

Eve struggled to undo the knots.

'For heavens' sake!' Knox took out his penknife and cut the string.

Unwrapped, it was a framed, abstract oil painting of fishes in shades of blue and green, from a pale duck egg to the deepest turquoise.

'I love it!' Eve, overcome, hugged Hester.

'Thank you. It's amazing.' Knox joined in.

Eve knew he was just being polite. He really wasn't interested in art, but feigned enthusiasm for her sake. She loved him for that.

She studied the blue-tinted fish drifting over the canvas, overlapping and twisting, their fins filmy, their scales translucent.

'It's like your style, darling,' noted Knox, to her surprise.

So it was. The painting had much in common with her oils of overlapping seashells in blues and greys hanging on the walls around them.

Hester caressed her gift. 'This is one amazing work of art.' She smiled. 'I really wanted to keep it for myself when I saw it, but I knew you'd love it too.'

Eve was studying the tiny signature. Her heart beat like a drum and she felt it must be audible to the others.

'Yes,' said Hester. 'It's an Alex Temple. After I had your email, I phoned some arty mates of mine and we tracked this down in a little East End gallery. His work's difficult to find. I only wish I'd had the foresight to buy some when I met him. But I was hard up then.'

'He didn't paint or sell much,' said Moussia. 'Too busy teaching to earn money.'

Eve just stared at the painting. 'I love it so much,' she said again.

July

There was no question of a honeymoon. For months Knox had spent long hours on his course and Eve had seen little of him. And he still had to work in his study. Then he had to go to London a few times for interviews with multinational companies to secure the job he wanted after graduation.

She felt despondent after Hester left. But every time she looked at the shimmering painting on the living room wall, she thought with pleasure of Alex Temple. She continued searching for information about him on the internet, but had little to go on. The Miansarows' memories helped, but her curiosity was insatiable. What sort of man had he been, exactly? Talented, yes. But kind? What was his relationship with her mother? Had he known about Eve?

Days passed as she had plenty to do putting the house to rights. Tom had almost finished tearing down partition walls and restoring the place to how it had been before the division into flats. All the major tasks were completed.

Her feelings of nausea had ended and she had her second scan at the city hospital. Knox was busy at the University, so she took Troy. Full of excitement over the train journey, he beamed out of the window, asking questions. 'What's that? Why's that stick going round? What's that tube for?'

He enjoyed the bus ride, too, and eventually they arrived at the hospital.

'I don't want to know whether it's a boy or girl,' she told the radiographer in the Maternity Outpatients' Ward.

'That's fine. Does your little boy want a brother or a sister?' The large woman scratched a mosquito bite on her ankle.

Eve felt surprise. Perhaps she hadn't considered Troy's feelings enough.

She lay back, her abdomen coated with jelly, and watched

images of her child moving on the screen. She marvelled at the roundness of the little head, the tiny bones of the spine, the waving hands and feet. It didn't seem possible to tell the sex, but Eve felt sure the expert would know.

'Look, Troy. That's the baby in my tummy.'

He stared, puzzled, at the blurry cloud formations on the screen, more interested in the woman's actions.

'What's she's doing?'

'I'm taking measurements of the head and stomach. Things like that,' said the woman. 'All seems normal.' She gave Eve a paper towel to wipe the jelly off, then handed her a copy of the black and white image.

On their return train journey to Shipden Eve talked to Troy about the baby growing in her abdomen.

He felt her stomach and put his ear against it. 'Him talking in there.' he said, after a minute.

'What's he saying?'

'You know, just rubbish.' He turned to her. 'Did I grow in yours tummy?'

She kissed his trusting face. 'No. You grew in Cheryl's tummy.'

'Cheryl cross,' he said, and turned to look out of the window again.

On Graduation Day at the University the sky over the coast darkened, heavy with thunderstorms. But the clouds passed out to sea.

Eve arranged for Moussia and Vlad to look after Troy. In the morning they arrived at the house with a small sailing ship that Vlad had carved for the boy to float on the boating pond.

'We show you.' Vlad's eyes gleamed with memories of his childhood, and Troy jumped up and down, eager to be off. Moussia had brought a picnic packed in a wicker basket for the three of them to have on the beach.

'Take these house keys,' said Eve. 'I'm not sure when we'll get back. Help yourself to anything.'

The ceremony passed in a blur of moving figures, capped and gowned. Eve hadn't seen Knox in this way before and admired him in his dramatic outfit. She felt intense pride in him, for his hard work and his achievement, and, for a brief moment, an impulse of envy.

'You've done so well.' She hugged him. 'Congratulations!' She insisted on taking numerous photos of him with his friends on the course.

She watched how he reacted to his friends and felt on the edge of the group until he told them he and Eve were married. Then, with shouts and kisses, arrangements were made to celebrate further in London later in the summer.

At the end of the afternoon, they drove back to Shipden through fields of wheat.

'That chapter's over,' said Knox with satisfaction. 'Now I can relax for a week before starting my new job. Though, to be honest, I'm looking forward to it. It'll be a challenge.'

He'd arranged to stay in tweed jacket man's flat as a paying guest during the week as it was near his firm's office. not far from Canary Wharf. 'Easy to get to from Liverpool Street Station. Dave's very easy-going. And I'll be home Friday evening until Monday morning. Not bad.'

He negotiated, with breathtaking ease on the winding road, overtaking a caravan line.

Eve gasped. 'I've a surprise tonight. We're going to the end of the pier show, you and I. It'll be a laugh. The old Russians will babysit. It's all fixed.'

She turned and saw him pulling a face. 'Must we? Surely not our sort of thing.'

'What is our sort of thing? It'll be fun. Something different. Escapism. It's a sort of modern version of the Victorian music hall.' She stifled her disappointment at his response.

He said no more, but at home poured himself a couple of large tumblers of whisky before they left.

'Priming yourself?'

He staggered on the walk down to the front and knocked against people in the crowd while getting to his seat.

No empty places showed in the small theatre. A noisy buzz of anticipation surrounded them.

'Lots of unsophisticated white heads here,' commented Knox loudly, turning round.

'Sh. Don't be so patronising. You don't know the extent of the worldliness in the audience. And as for white hair, just think how stylish the Miansarows are.'

'That's true.'

'You'll be an old git, too, one of these days,' she whispered.

'Don't remind me. I'm already getting the odd grey hair and I'm just in my prime.' He yawned loudly. 'Come on, let's get this over with.'

Eve thought of black-thatched Choker. What would he make of this variety show? He'd probably been to all the end of the pier shows in Shipden since he'd lived there. He was open to every experience. She wondered where he was and what he could be doing. Writing, probably, staring into space or striding about, trying to find exactness. The precise words to convey his meaning. She remembered him saying, 'A good poem is elusive. It slips away like a dream and you have to be quick to catch it.' She shivered in the warm theatre.

The musicians struck up, and shortly after the red curtains rose to enthusiastic applause. The people in the audience were regular pier theatregoers and knew what to expect.

It turned out to be an old-fashioned music hall variety show catering for all tastes. There was lots of harsh noise and vivid, hot colours. The comedian who was used to cabaret, had instant likeability and seemed well able to entertain all age groups. Eve and even Knox, to his surprise, found themselves laughing aloud at the odd jokes. The singers belting out past hits, the jazz musicians, illusionists, trapeze artistes and stylish dancers all showed enthusiasm. Eve thought that the good-looking, talented entertainers had been chosen to appeal to every single person in the audience. She particularly admired a tall, dark male dancer who seemed to wink at her alone while performing as a Ukrainian Cossack. No doubt gay, she guessed. Knox had eyes only for a little blonde chorus girl.

As they came out at the end, she gripped his hand. They joined the celebratory crowd streaming along the pier under the swaying-coloured lights.

'It wasn't so bad, was it?'

'No. I have to admit I quite enjoyed it. That comedian reminded me of a mate of mine in the Gulf.'

'That cackling woman behind us sounded as though she was laying an egg.'

Back at the house, the old couple were yawning and ready to go home in their taxi.

'Troy, he sleep good. Very tired, wearing us out. He like his metal bed with soldiers on,' said Moussia.

'Yes, it's new. He chose it,' said Knox. 'When we got back from the shop, he studied our antique double bed and told us, "Yours bed has meat pots".'

'I suppose he means those metal finials on the corners. They must look like tins of corned beef or Spam to him. Funny child.' Eve went to check on him.

When she returned Knox was finishing the whisky.

'You're going at the alcohol these days.'

'Don't bloody nag. It helps me sleep.'

They went silently to their meat pot bed.

August

The colony of terns shrieked in unmusical chorus. 'Kirrikirri kit kit kirr,' in high-pitched screams. A protective clamour.

'Stink,' said Troy, holding his nose as the boat passed the sandy strip of shingle where the birds nested on the ground. The passengers watched the terns diving and fluttering. They commented on the birds' red legs and orange-red bills with black tips, but Troy was unimpressed.

As the boat swung round in the choppy sea, a wave came over the side and splashed Knox's fleece. He swore. The other tourist passengers looked away.

Troy gave him a sharp stare. The boat chugged on.

'See.' Eve pointed ahead. 'There they are. That's what we've come to see, they're called common or grey seals.'

The little boy stood for a good view as they neared the beach where the fat creatures lay, moving flippers and opening their eyes. The seals didn't move away but stared at the intruders with disinterest.

Troy's mouth dropped open. 'Let's go and kick em,' he said.

Knox laughed.

A large seal surfaced near the boat. Its dog head reared up and scorn showed in its eyes.

Troy sat quickly and clutched Eve's hand. 'They big, those old seals.'

The rest of the trip was uneventful. The water rippled in the glare.

Back on the marshes everyone disembarked. The breeze they'd felt at sea dropped on land and heat trembled from the dry, stony path and stubbly grass. Eve's lips tasted salty. Knox carried his damp fleece to the car.

'That was a good trip,' Eve said. 'When we get home, let's go for a swim.'

As they drove back, Troy sat silently watching the crops being harvested. Giant golden straw bales filled the fields. Orchards showed plums, apples and pears ripening and hedges full of early blackberries. At last he spoke, 'At ours beach,' he gave a gusty sigh, 'do those old seals go there?'

'No,' said Eve. 'They don't like to swim too near people.'

'Good,' said Troy.

She felt tired as she often did, sighing with heartburn. Swimming would be good. Then she was conscious of a wave like movement spreading across her front and visualised her infant squirming inside. I am growing my own child, she thought happily, and stroked her stomach.

Knox noticed. 'You all right, darling?'

'Absolutely.'

'You sure swimming's a good idea?' He briefly patted her thigh.

'Yes. It's fine. I'm fine.' She stared at his strong profile and long neck. Then turned to the back seat.

'What's yours baby called, in yours stomach?' Troy asked, screwing his face like a little old man.

'No name, yet.'

'We could call him Karl,' said Knox.

'It might be a girl.' Eve wanted a surprise.

'Pencil,' suggested Troy. 'Or caterpillar.' The last time he'd been on the beach, he'd made a giant caterpillar of sand with flintstone eyes. A fierce monster.

'Possibly,' said Eve. 'Let's wait and see what the baby looks like.'

'Frog,' said Troy. 'Racing car. Tweezer.'

They drove back in silence, reflecting.

In Shipden when the tide was out, she and Troy often walked along the beach, paddling in the sea. She felt close to him, felt she knew what he was thinking, as they breathed in the soft, salty air, listened to the sky larks singing above the cliffs, felt the sand firm below and ripples breaking over their feet.

While Troy ambled beside her, absorbed in towing his little boat on a piece of string one day, she thought of her mother, that dominating figure who had been so careless with her affection and only child. Eve remembered her anxieties when she stayed with her mother. The long hours she waited for her to come home, waited to see what state she was in, without understanding. The woman had, at times, been liable to stagger about and lie on the floor insensible for hours, then wake bad-tempered. At those times, Eve could do nothing right. If there was money in the purse, she could buy bread, cereal and milk.

Sometimes, her mother would come home, pull off her clothes and tell Eve to run her a bath. The child obeyed, careful to test that the water wasn't too hot. Her mother would somehow manage to climb into the bath, clinging to the walls, then subside, groaning. Later she would usually prove too uncoordinated to get out and small Eve would tug and heave, uselessly, to the accompaniment of curses. Her mother would have to stay in the empty bath, being dried with a towel and covered with a quilt, until she was sober enough to get herself over the edge.

Eve remembered feeling anger towards her mother, knowing the woman couldn't be trusted, a person who said one thing and did another, who made promises she didn't keep. Yet Eve had loved her, so much. Her only family.

Somehow, recalling things in that tranquil beach setting helped her to put memories in order, firmly in the past. She knew there were happier times to come.

One Sunday evening Knox was lying on the sofa watching a documentary while Eve cleared their mugs. As she passed behind him, seeing his sandy hair sticking in a funny tuft, she felt a great surge of affection and ruffled his hair.

'Don't damned well do that,' he snapped. 'I don't like my

hair touched.'

She froze, her hand still stretched towards him. A chill descended on her. With difficulty she moved away into the kitchen.

Had her pregnancy made her more sensitive to criticism? Was the magic wearing off for him? They had spent months, it seemed, in each other's arms. What was the matter with him? Or, rather, what was the matter with her? What had she done to annoy him? She was irrevocably hurt. This was rejection. The spite in his voice cut. She said nothing, but stood at the sink washing up mechanically, allowing a nugget of bitterness and resentment to grow. When she'd finished, she called to him, 'I'm just going for a walk.'

He grunted.

She checked on Troy asleep in bed. Even though it was late, she left the house and walked through the town. It was a warm night and a few young holidaymakers in flimsy clothes were still about, giggling from benches and doorways. She went along the front above the cliffs past the lit-up hotels where no one was about. An occasional car sped down the road. She felt alone, sad. She held her hands under her bump for comfort, wondering about her baby.

Then she felt a twinge of sexual desire and thought again about Knox. Perhaps the stress of his new job was affecting him. She needed a man's arms. She stopped and stared out to the dimly lit sea that swished rhythmically below. Then turned, resting against the railings. She saw a man at a second-floor hotel window also gazing at the sea. He had his back to the lamplight so she could only see his dark shape, tall and broad shouldered.

She shivered in her thin muslin dress. He blew a puff of smoke towards her out of the open window. She knew he was staring at her now. He stubbed his cigarette on the windowsill and threw the butt out. She dropped her glance. When she looked up, he turned and went out of the room, shutting off the light. She imagined him running down two flights of stairs and out of the front door to come after her.

At once afraid, she hurried away as fast as she could go, keeping in the shadows until she reached home.

Unsettled, she prepared for bed. Knox was there already, snoring slightly.

Aware he had to be up early the next day, she crept carefully in beside him in the gloom. He stirred and moved nearer to her. 'You're cold,' he muttered sleepily, his fingers fumbling along her thighs.

As always, she enjoyed the sex, but this time it was a clinical business lacking the sweetness of emotion.

Afterwards for a long time she lay in the dark, troubled, unable to sleep.

At weekends, they had good days as Knox took the family for trips to different places. But there were times when he became easily irritated and refused to talk about the change in his temperament.

'How are you feeling now?' asked Eve one Sunday, after he'd spent the morning reading the papers.

'Fine. Why do you ask?' He threw the papers on the floor.

'You seemed a bit on edge at breakfast.'

'What d'you mean "on edge"? I'm always calm and rational.' His voice rose. 'And what's that stupid look for?'

'I don't think you are always calm. Sometimes you seem testy and stressed. Like this morning.'

'I was perfectly fine this morning,' he said loudly.

'You shouted at Troy for leaving his cars on the stairs. The coffee I made was too hot for you. The toast apparently overdone. You swore at the milk jug. Then went in the living room and slammed the door.' She paused. 'That's what I meant by being on edge. Irritable. So Troy and I left you alone.'

'Good God, woman. You don't know the meaning of the

expression "on edge". You don't understand what real stress is. You've had an easy time of it.'

'I could disagree with that. Look, is there something wrong, Knox?' She put her arm round him.

'Yes, there damned well is. It's you, winding me up all the time. I can do without it. Just leave me alone.' He shrugged her arm off. 'I don't want to talk to you at all. Get out of my hair.' His expression was bitter, closed.

She persisted. 'I'm just wondering if you're ill. You were walking in your sleep last night. You got out of bed and wandered down the landing, then came back to bed. When I spoke to you, you didn't answer and I realised you were still asleep. Is something preying on you? It's better if we share.'

'I don't want to share anything with you.'

The scent of roasted meat reached them. 'Lunch is almost ready,' she said.

'I don't want any. It's too hot for cooked stuff. I just want you to mind your own business.' He walked out of the room. 'I'm going to London now. I've got too much to do there. I'll just get my kit.' The door banged behind him.

She heard him running upstairs. There's something badly wrong, she thought. I'm behaving no differently from the way I've always been.

It had been a struggle to stop herself losing her temper and shouting at him. That's the easy way out, she decided, being as bad tempered as him. It doesn't do any good, and would frighten Troy. She felt virtuous keeping quiet and wanted to keep calm for the baby's sake, but her heart raced. She wanted to be sick. She recalled the old anxieties, confusions.

'Troy,' she called, 'lunchtime.'

He came running with a toy car in each hand. Anything with wheels would keep him absorbed for long periods. He sat on a chair with a fat cushion to bring him level with the table, and watched as she carved the joint, giving him two thin slices and cutting them up on his plate.

'Five potatoes, please,' he said.

'Can you eat as many as that?'

'Yes. Lots like Knox. He's late.' Troy twisted round to look for him.

They listened as the front door slammed and the car engine rumbled on the drive.

'He didn't say "goodbye".' The boy's expression showed outrage.

'He's in a hurry. Never mind. Eat up your meat. It's your favourite.'

'If you give me lots, I'll be yours friend.'

'I thought I was always your friend, anyway.'

He paused in his chewing and thought.

She laughed and kissed the top of his head.

'Yes. I am yours friend,' he said.

'Good.'

A breeze sprang up and jangled the wind chimes outside the window. 'Our new bells are crying,' said Troy.

Later that week the social worker called again. She sat in the kitchen drinking a mug of coffee. Her face sagged into lines of exhaustion.

'It's Troy's Nanny,' she said, glancing at the hall where the boy ran around, out of earshot, absorbed in being a train.

'Is she any better?' asked Eve.

'No. That's the trouble. The cancer's advanced too far. She can't last much longer. I don't think Troy should see her at the hospice. She's too ill.'

'I'm sorry. She always seemed fond of him.'

'Does he ever mention her or his mother?'

'Neither. Not for a long time.'

'He appears to be happy here.' The social worker smiled unexpectedly. 'We're glad you're looking after him. Your police check was fine and your social service assessment is going well. We consider you suitable for fostering. He does need a lot of attention. And, to be honest, there's nowhere else for him to go. And Cheryl's younger brothers have disappeared. They were into drugs, too.' She pushed a hand through her hair. 'There's a big shortage of foster carers in this county. Every year the social services here help around ten thousand children and youngsters and nearly a thousand are in foster care. We try to keep them in their familiar areas and give them plenty of support. As a carer you'll get help, training and an allowance. We'll be there for you twenty-four hours a day.'

Eve poured more coffee. 'You know we want to adopt Troy.'

'I remember. I'm sure that'll be okay. We can set the wheels in motion. I'll talk about it again to my boss, Mrs Abbott.'

That must be the pangolin, thought Eve. 'And I'd be happy to foster other children here. There's plenty of room.'

'That would be great. We're desperate for approved foster parents in this town. But it's not easy, you know. We may have to call you in the middle of the night to take kids when crimes are involved. And children can come for one night, or months or years. You never know. They can be babies, teen Mums, all ages. They may not even speak English. Their parents can come and visit, or say they're coming and never turn up. The children may have had difficult lives. They usually need a lot of help. But our aim is to get kids back to their families eventually.'

'I feel I could do good.' But as she said it, Eve felt doubts. 'I'll do my best, anyway. My foster parents made a world of difference to my life. They were kind and considerate. They're gone now. But I'd like to make a difference to some children's lives. As they did to mine.'

'You'd never know who would turn up for breakfast. Abused kids can be difficult. They need a lot. You'd not just have to feed them; you'd have to have patience. You need a big commitment to kids.' She stared into Eve's eyes. 'We can put your fostering on an official footing. The team manager will come and see you and tell you all about it. I can't say when, we've a shortage of trained social workers. You and your husband can fill in some more forms.' She collected her papers. 'I must go. But I'll drop by again soon.'

September

The sea thrashed angrily against the legs of the pier. Off to the side, gulls rode the waves calmly, their tail feathers sticking up like bits of wood.

Eve moved slowly against the wind, heavy and awkward, her shopping in plastic bags bumping against her legs as she trudged the slope from the sea.

She went to collect Troy from his nursery school. He'd started going two mornings a week and enjoyed it so much she decided to increase his sessions.

'So, how was it today?' she asked him as they walked back to the house.

'Bit boring. I have winned something. We did sticking. I did have to stick a house and I spilled my milk.' He stopped and looked up at her. 'But nobody was cross.'

'That's good. I expect it was an accident. Did you see your new friends, Emily and Joel?'

'We played in the Wendy House. At cooking. I be'd Knox, shouting.'

'He doesn't often shout,' she said, thinking that he never did until recently.

They turned off the pavement towards their front door.

'Where's Cherl?' His voice was sharp and clear.

Taken aback, she put down her shopping and searched for her key. 'She's gone to live with your Nanny in Heaven. We won't see them anymore.'

'Cherl dropped ketchup on the floor and Nanny said "stupid cow" and Cherl said it, too.'

'Those things don't matter where they are now. Let's go and see if your new tractor is in the kitchen where you left it.'

He ran ahead of her through the hall. 'Yes, it isn't runned away.'

'Would you like fish or tomato soup?'

'Tomatoes. Soup is yuk. Stupid cow.'

Pretending she didn't hear, she put the shopping away.

Later that evening, long after Troy had fallen asleep, Eve was laboriously knitting a multicoloured baby blanket when the phone rang.

'It's me.' Knox's voice coming through space always had a hint of a Scottish accent, which wasn't noticeable face-to-face.

'How are things?' she asked warily, ready to make excuses to herself about his struggle with the responsibilities of his new job.

'Better this week. I'm beginning to understand how the company works. The politics and so on.' He yawned. 'What're you up to?'

'Nothing much. Trying to knit. The first time since I learned how to do it aged nine. I'm hopeless. I've bought huge needles and great fat balls of wool. It's a little blanket. Hardly a masterpiece. I keep dropping stitches. You'll laugh when you see it.'

'No, I won't. The thing is, Eve, I'm ringing to apologise. I know I've been a real bastard to you recently. Not explaining things. Being foul. But I didn't want to worry you.' He paused. 'The fact is that Dad's money ran out a while ago. Buying all the flats and putting the house back together cost more than I planned. Being in debt and jobless was terrifying. And then I didn't think I could fit in with this company. I've been expecting the sack every day.' He was tired. 'But this morning the Managing Director *praised* my work. I feel better about everything.'

'Knox, I'm so glad. But I wish you'd told me how you felt. We could have talked. I would have understood. I'm your wife and I care about you.' She sighed. 'We needn't have done so much to the house so soon. I can go back to work.'

'I don't want you to do that. I need you to stay home

finishing off the jobs in the house. I'd have to pay someone to do that, otherwise. And you have to care for Troy and the new baby coming. And you want to foster children.'

'We'll get paid for that. I wouldn't want you to be out of pocket.'

'No. I reckon I should be able to pay all the outstanding bills in the next few months. I was just suffering a crisis of confidence.'

Long after they'd finished talking and hung up, she sat in the dark watching the uncurtained rectangle of flickering orange street lights. In the other direction at sea, dots of light moved over the blackness. Traffic passed fitfully on the road beyond the rose bushes and old flint wall. As a motorbike droned past, she thought briefly of Choker. Where was he? What was he doing? Would she ever see him again?

Her baby stirred. She smiled to herself. Soon, a matter of weeks, she would see this much-wanted child.

And perhaps things would be better with Knox now he'd told her what had been troubling him. They must certainly talk more, communicate properly in those weekends when they had the chance. She wanted to know all about his childhood. He'd never been able to tell her about it, or about his mysterious mother who'd left his father when Knox was small. Eve needed to learn everything. And to unburden herself by telling him every detail there was to know about herself, too.

At last, standing, she turned on the lights and drew the curtains. Heavy pale stuff that hung in regal folds. She stroked the surface with pleasure.

Pinned on one wall were sketches of Troy she'd done earlier, when he was absorbed in his play with toy lorries. It was always the nape of his neck looking so vulnerable that touched her most. She felt love for him and pity, mixed with the occasional flare of disappointment.

'I don't like you,' he'd said.

'Why's that?' She chewed the end of her pencil.

'I don't. I don't like William and I don't like Emily at my Nursery.'

'Yes, you do. Anyway, I like you.' She went back to her drawing.

He put his lorries in their shoebox garage, then lay face down on the rug, jiggling about in a frenzy.

'What are you doing?' She smiled.

He lifted his head. 'I'm pinging my legs.'

'Is that good?'

'You ping yours legs.' He jumped up and took her hand.

She lay on her back and shook her limbs, saying, 'I'm not pinging too much because I don't want to upset the baby.'

He went back to his lorries. 'I like you now,' he said.

Dear Eve,

It seems an age since I last emailed you. I'm in the Slough of Despond having had some hellish bad luck. My bloody publishers aren't doing my book after all. It's just so sickening after the work I've done on it, and the encouragement I'd been given. They'd been prevaricating for months and finally said yesterday that they'd had a change of heart because Hugo wasn't famous enough. It's all rubbish. They'd loved all my descriptions of the hard-drinking Colony Rooms set who gathered round Francis Bacon. Of course, Hugo would be better known if they'd published my flaming book.

I'm sick of living in London. To be honest, it's lonely here in the flat without Choker. And my old so-called friends are getting so bloody decrepit they won't go out at night for fear of getting mugged. Pluto's pining for long walks on the marshes, too. So you'll not be surprised to hear I'm coming back to Shipden where my real friends are. Choker put his bits and pieces in store and buggered off to Peru. He finally sent me a postcard. Anyway, I'm selling the flat, putting my furniture in store too and coming to stay with Vlad and Moussia until I can find a little place to buy in Shipden. Property's gone up in the short time I've been here, so I should be in profit. Would you like help with all those children you intend to care for? I'm really looking forward to seeing you and Troy. Not forgetting Knox. I thought he might call in on me one day, but I expect he's very busy with his new job.

I've been clearing out my stuff and came across an old bottle of my favourite perfume, Shocking de Schiaparelli. Breathing in the trace of scent made me so nostalgic. I listened to Charles Trenet singing La Mer, and wept buckets. I'm ready for a change.

Eve, I have a surprise. I've been beavering away on your behalf, ringing up old contacts, and finally come up with a telephone number for Alex Temple's sister. She's pretty ancient, called June Parsons, and staying in South Africa at the moment but will be home in north London at the end of February. Apparently, she's small, fair, blue-eyed, artistic, and walks in knock-kneed fashion. Remind you of anyone? She may have off-spring. Who knows?

That's all for now. Affectionately, Hester.

The sun glared on the lighthouse from a deep blue sky. Eve, Hester and Troy, enjoying the warmth, walked slowly through fields and woods above the cliffs. The two women sat on a bench and Eve thankfully put her feet up. Troy ran back and forth and round them like a puppy, bringing found treasures: special sticks, stones and yellowing leaves.

'It's just an answer phone message on June Parson's number. It's a pity she's not back for weeks. I'm so curious about her,' said Eve.

'You'll just have to hold your horses. There's no way of contacting her until she gets home.' Hester lit up. 'I've tried acupuncture and hypnotism to stop this wretched smoking. In vain. It's nicotine patches next. My addiction's too expensive,' she wheezed.

'Good luck with it.' Eve looked at her watch. 'We'll have to get back soon. The men are bringing us those sets of bunk beds this afternoon.' She called to Troy. 'You can watch them carry the beds upstairs and set them up.'

'Yes.' He jumped around.

Hester inhaled deeply. 'Then you'll be ready for the children when Mrs Abbott gives you the call.'

'That's right. I'm getting excited about it. I went through the application process ages ago, I've done the training courses and we've been approved as foster parents. We're just waiting for what they call the first "placement".' She put a hand on her front where the baby was kicking strongly. 'There was something I wanted to tell you about. A strange thing. The other day I was coming downstairs from my studio and heard a sighing. For a second I thought I saw Amos standing on the landing outside his old door. A sort of misty sensation, not frightening at all. Most odd. Because I'm cynical. Don't believe in ghostly sightings.' She paused. 'I always felt pity for him.'

'Poor sod. He didn't have much happiness in his life. I always thought he really liked you.'

'He enjoyed your parties.'

'That's true. I did hear him laughing then.' Hester blew a slow smoke ring. 'Perhaps he'll just be a benign presence in the house.'

'Perhaps.'

Half an hour later as they turned the corner near the house, they saw a police car drive off the road and park next to Eve's front door.

'Look!' shouted Troy with excitement. He ran for home.

Eve and Hester exchanged a glance and hurried after him.

Two uniformed police officers stepped out of the car. The woman rang the doorbell.

'That's ours house,' Troy shouted at them as he approached the car.

The officers turned. 'Are you Mrs Smith?' the man asked Eve. He didn't smile.

'Yes.' A cold dread seeped through her.

'May we come in?'

She nodded, fumbled in her bag for her key, unlocked the door then led the way into the hall.

The young woman looked at Hester. 'Could you take the little boy and make some tea, please?'

As they disappeared silently into the kitchen, Eve went into the living room and sat. Her legs felt shaky.

She was aware of the officers sitting next to her and talking slowly, of the sympathy in the young woman's eyes and of a hand in hers. The truth of what they were saying came gradually into her understanding. As it did so, she cried out and the world whirled away from her into darkness.

October

She woke and momentarily couldn't think where she could be. Aching with discomfort, she remembered. This was a small, pale painted room with a smell of disinfectant. In a plastic crib like a fish tank beside her hospital bed lay a newborn baby. This was her own child, asleep. The baby's hair was black against the white sheet, her face very pink and crumpled.

Eve recalled what had happened, and wept. First in sadness for Knox, who had gone. And next happiness in her child whose swift arrival had been caused by the shock of hearing of the tragedy.

There had been a fire at night in the London flat where Knox was staying. It had probably started in a defective old tumble drier. The battery in the smoke alarm needed replacing and Knox, alone and fast asleep, had died from smoke inhalation.

Knox, I miss you so much, Eve thought. You should be here with your arms around me, filled with joy at the sight of this child. I need you so much. And now I'm alone again. I can't bear it. Alone to bring up another little girl without a father. Am I cursed or something?

The door opened and Hester's unkempt head appeared round it. 'Are you receiving visitors?'

Eve blotted her face with tissues and smiled as Troy came in, staggering under the weight of a huge bouquet of pink carnations. 'Here,' he said, dumping the flowers on her bed and climbing up to give her a kiss. 'Is yours baby out yet?'

'Yes. Look, there she is.'

He leaned over. 'She's small.' He sounded disappointed.

'She'll grow,' said Hester. 'I think she's absolutely beautiful. You're very clever, Eve. Well done. What are you going to call her?'

'Angela, after my mother.' Eve put her arm round Troy to stop him falling off the bed. 'She made mistakes with me. She wasn't good with children, but I forgave her a million times over once I became a young mother myself. I realised it's a hard thing, parenting, it's a huge responsibility to create and bring up a child. I've been thinking a lot about my mother and I'm sure she really did want me after all.'

Hester hugged her. 'Of course she did. You're very loveable.' Then she touched Angela's soft cheek. 'What a mop of hair. Not red then.'

'No.' Eve stared out of the window into the far distance. She seemed lost. 'There were three of us. Now there are three again and I don't know what to do. I'm worried about the house. I'll have to go back to living in my little flat and there's not much room there for Angela, Troy and me.'

'Whatever are you talking about? Knox was your husband. Remember, the whole house was in both your names. It all belongs to you now. We all talked about his will one night at supper. You don't need to worry about anything. He's left you well provided for, I'm sure.' She picked up the flowers. 'I'll go and find a vase for these.'

A fortnight later, Eve took Troy to nursery school, then went along the front pushing Angela, well tucked with blankets against the cold wind from the north, in her new buggy.

The tide was high and great waves crashed noisily against the concrete walls. Further down the beach, fragments of blown white spume flew up and rolled along the sand. The sea, grey and greasy, tormented by the wind, showed angry white caps.

Eve could see, down the coast, the village two miles away, where the driven waves were breaking over the sea wall in curtains rising and falling. In the eerie mistiness, so close to the crashing waves, she could smell seaweed and salt. The crab boats were pulled high on the shingle and gulls wheeled silently above in the great, empty sky.

If only seawater could cure all ailments, she thought. The high cupolas above seemed foreign and for the first time she saw the church on the cliff, appearing as a frightened rabbit with high pointed ears and buckteeth. There was no one about. Turning, she walked quickly in the breeze as she struggled up the concrete slope and along the cliff edge out of town. In her bag, hanging from the buggy, was a great bunch of copper chrysanthemums issuing a sharp, metallic scent.

Am I running from God, or towards him? She asked herself. I don't know what I'm doing.

At the little cemetery on top of the hill she bumped the buggy over the wet grass until she reached Knox's grave. Only the fresh dug earth marked the place where he had so recently been buried. The headstone would come later when the soil settled. Carefully she filled the container there with water and placed the chrysanthemums in it. As she stood, thinking of Knox, her head bowed and tears dripping from her face, a hesitant rain began. She was conscious of the leaves on the small, sparse trees changing colour, from green to ochre to red, and blowing away. Everything was changing for her. She pulled the buggy hood and waterproof tight and hurried home.

An easterly gale began screeching. On the cliffs, she heard the rumble of breakers before she saw the great racing waves swelling with seething crests. The silver, slanting rain stopped and the wind howled, shrieked and buffeted the houses in the steely light.

As she approached her house, Angela cried, miserable high-pitched whimpers, and at the same time Eve saw the social worker's car parked outside.

Mrs Abbot wound down her window. 'Filthy weather,' she called. 'May I come in?'

Not now, Eve thought; I saw you only two days ago. But she beckoned the woman, hung up her own soaking mackintosh, and extricated Angela from the buggy. 'Do you mind if I feed the baby while we're talking?'

'Go ahead. She sounds hungry.'

Settled in an armchair, her blouse undone, and Angela quiet at her breast, Eve felt calmer.

'I want to congratulate you on Troy. He's a real credit to you. You've given him a stability he never had before.' Mrs Abbot's voice was confident, but she wrung her hands.

'I don't know about that. But he's a lovely child. Good-tempered. I can hardly remember the time before he lived with me.' With us, she thought. Knox gave, too.

'Is he jealous of the baby?'

'He doesn't show any sign of that. When Hester brought us home from the hospital, I gave Troy a little train set and told him that it was a present from Angela. He approves of her.'

Mrs Abbot picked up her file. 'Congratulations. It's all fixed. The adoption and the fostering. We had to run checks on you, you understand, for everyone's good. Everything's been done. You're approved.' She sighed. 'I didn't really want to load you up with work so soon, but we have a problem. We urgently need a place for a thirteen-year-old girl. There's nowhere else for her to stay. And she goes to the local secondary school. We don't want her to have to change schools. She has enough problems. Could you cope meantime? Until I sort something else out for the poor soul?' Her eyes were sharp.

What does it matter? thought Eve. It's better when I'm busy, then there's less time to think. 'Yes, that's fine. The bedrooms are finished now and a friend, Vlad, has fixed wooden bars at the bottom of the windows. Everything's safe. What's the girl called?'

'Gabby Pilgrim. She's quiet. Her mother's just been sectioned and I think will be in the psychiatric hospital some time. There are no known relatives. The two of them have been living in the back of beyond, at least a mile down a tractor track. No houses round about. Gabby walks through the fields to the nearest road to catch the school bus. She'll enjoy living so near school.' Mrs Abbot smiled. 'That's a relief. Thanks for agreeing. I'll go and get her now. A colleague is looking after her in my office.' She got to her feet with difficulty. 'Don't move, I'll see myself out. I won't be long. If Gabby's not up to school for a bit, that's okay. She's had a shock.'

I know what it's like, thought Eve, watching Angela feeding. The baby's blue eyes regarded her own steadily, glazed with contentment. Eve felt great love towards the little creature. She and Troy look very similar, she realised, without surprise. And Jez, too.

She kissed the infant where her soft face curved into her soft neck.

Later, Angela asleep in her cot, Eve cleaned a bedroom for the girl and sorted out bed linen. She unexpectedly caught sight of herself in the small mirror and was taken aback at her gaunt appearance, her long hair meagre and her expression weary and somehow blank.

The doorbell rang. Mrs Abbot stood there, serene, her hand on the child's shoulder. 'This is Gabby, Mrs Smith. I'm afraid I can't stop, I've a big case load. Some urgent matters. I'll ring you tonight. Sorry I have to rush.' And she jumped in her car and drove off without a backward glance.

In the hall Eve and Gabby studied each other. The girl seemed small for her age, with thin limbs and body and a disproportionately large, round head with light, tangled hair hanging over her spectacles. She wore broken-down, filthy trainers, torn jeans and a grey hooded sweat top. Her eyes were wary. She reminded Eve of herself at thirteen.

Eve hugged her. 'You can call me Eve.' She picked up the bag the social worker had dropped. 'What's in here?'

'Me school uniform and spare clothes.'

Not much there. 'That's good. Come with me and I'll show you your room.'

Upstairs, Gabby stared at the bunk beds. 'Can I have the top one?'

'Whichever you want. This is just your room. Would you like the lilac duvet cover or the green one?'

'That one.' Together they put the lilac cover on the bed.

'I'll leave you to put your things away in the drawers here, and in the wardrobe. Then we'll have something to eat. Here's your towel and the bathroom's next door.'

Gabby took an old toy bear out of the bag and put it on her pillow. 'You got other kids here?'

'Just my little boy, Troy. He's three now. And my new baby, Angela.'

The girl's face registered no emotion. She emptied the few garments from the bag onto the floor.

Eve went downstairs. We'll have to go shopping to get some more clothes for Gabby, she thought. She'll enjoy that.

With a little click, a post card came through the letterbox and fell on the mat. The shadow of the postman slid across the glass in the door and disappeared.

She picked up the card which showed a view of Machu Picchu. She studied the unfamiliar shapes of the white, wraithlike, lost city of the Incas, the numerous steps of the citadel and the vivid, spinach-green trees. I don't know anyone who's in the Andes, she thought. Slowly she turned the card over.

Hope all is well with you, Beauty. I'm coming back to England next month. As I have some unfinished business I intend to call on you in Shipden. For some reason I can't stop writing about humming-birds and you. C.

It was Choker's unmistakeable jagged handwriting in thick black ink.

She stared out of the window at the sea continually swallowing its secrets. 'Look at the sea and remember me,' he'd once told her.

From outside came the desolate cry of the wind. She looked at the card again. And as she did so the sun streamed through the window and its warmth made her smile.